For Our Children

ALICE'S ADVENTURES IN WONDERLAND

LEWIS CARROLL'S

Illustrated by Barry Moser. Preface and Notes by

James R. Kincaid. Text edited by Selwyn H. Goodacre.

Harcourt Brace Jovanovich, Publishers

New York San Diego London

HBJ

Library of Congress Cataloging-in-Publication Data
Carroll, Lewis, 1832–1898.
[Alice's adventures in Wonderland]
Lewis Carroll's Alice's adventures in Wonderland/illustrated
by Barry Moser: preface and notes by James R. Kincaid:
text edited by Selwyn H. Goodacre.
p. cm.
Summary: A little girl falls down a rabbit hole and discovers a
world of nonsensical and amusing characters.
ISBN 0-15-104230-6. — ISBN 0-15-604426-9 (A Harvest/HBJ book: pbk.)
[1. Fantasy.] I. Moser, Barry, ill. II. Goodacre, Selwyn Hugh.
III. Title. IV. Title: Alice's adventures in Wonderland.
[PZ7.D684Ap 1991]
[Fic]—dc20 91-26343

Printed in the United States of America

A B C D E

CONTENTS

PREFACE

There is a quaint and pristine Victorian phrase that describes with precision *Alice in Wonderland* and its relation to our culture: "We don't know where to have it." How do we locate this work, hold it still? Do we have it for adults, for children, for psychoanalysts, for mathematicians, for logicians, for linguists, for philosophers, for literary critics, for tea? Perhaps the last suggestion is most appropriate, since Alice and her readers are entering a world in which, as no less an authority than the Mad Hatter announces, "It's always tea-time!": a perpetual party for receptive children.

But children, receptive or dull, are not so clearly the work's only, or even major, audience. Carroll originally wanted as a title, *Alice's Golden Hours*, suggestive of such a restricted readership and of a fawning sentimentality the book, happily, seldom achieves. He preferred *Alice's Adventures in Wonderland*, he said, because it is "sensational." One might also add that the second title is cooler, less committed to the heroine and to the closed world of children's literature. In any event, the work clearly takes sensational risks, issuing attacks and invitations in all directions. Most of us find the means to desensitize ourselves to literary attacks and to exaggerate our capacities to fit the terms of the invitations. Still, *Alice in Wonderland* is, in this regard, an uncommonly capacious book.

How is it that this apparently innocent children's story is so hospitable, seeming to welcome a nearly unlimited number of approaches and explanations? The amount of commentary is considerable but less striking than its wild variety (the variety less striking than the wildness): the directly contradictory force of separate, by-themselves-perfectly-plausible analyses. No wizard could make all these readings cohere or arrange them as searchlights shining from different angles on the same work. Most often, the searchlights are beamed straight at one another. It makes one wonder where the work is–whether there is only one work or many–or none. Carroll himself provided a suggestive commentary on this phenomenon. When asked what one of his works meant, he would answer either that he had no idea or else give a fuller version of what is, after all, the same response: "Words mean more than we mean to express when we use them: so a whole book ought to mean a great deal more than the writer meant." In a book like *Alice in Wonderland*, which defies ordinary reading conventions, the fluidity Carroll talks of becomes a torrent. The book opens itself to all sorts of models: it is a satire, a novel, a mathematical-political-logical-theological allegory, a dream vision, and an elegy all at once; both a comedy and an irony; a work with rich and directed meaning and one without any whatever. Again, Carroll gives the best and most sophisticated explanation: "*Do* we decide questions at all? We decide *answers*, no doubt, but surely the questions decide *us*." Questions not only precede answers; questions determine answers. More to the point, "questions decide *us*." We are what we ask.

No work is directed more relentlessly or with more subtlety to the questions we habitually ask, the models we use to structure, understand, and make bearable our world and our lives. Carroll applies continuous pressure to the forms and models we use to think about such things as space, time, logic, language, meaning, authority, and death. Under such pressure, these structures explode, their naturalness disappears, and only the paltry skin remains. Without the desperate puffing which inflates them, the models are not there. Nor are they wanted. The anarchic creatures in equally anarchic Wonderland seem not to share our need for these props, the ones we are, incidentally, so very eager to thrust upon children.

Alice, interestingly, is distinctly uncomfortable without these supports. Early on, when she finds herself so disoriented by the fall down the rabbit-hole that she forgets who she is, she tries to regain her identity by reconstructing her above-ground culture and placing herself in it. One of her strategies involves the effort to recite moralistic and didactic poems in an attempt to recapture official cultural statements, adult versions of what is going on and adult instructions on how to behave and think. In this case, she goes after a particularly grisly example, Isaac Watts's "Against Idleness and Mischief" ("How doth the little busy bee"). Bees are held up to children as a behavioral and epistemological model, a model of unremitting labor that had better be followed unblinkingly, since "Satan finds some mischief still / For idle hands to do." Spending one's life avoiding idleness will pay off in the end, when one will be able to "give for every day / Some good account at last" to the great Bookkeeper in the skies. In Wonderland, however, such notions are so alien – one is reminded of Harold Skimpole's witty protest against the dratted bees (*Bleak House*, ch.8) – that Alice finds herself, against her will, exploding with a wonderful and subversive parody where the industrious bees are replaced by the indolent but remarkably successful crocodile.

Watts's poem offers a highly ordered and highly sentimental view in which Man and Nature – bees, at least – are joined harmoniously through God's plan. The animal kingdom is a benign example for us all; and the ruling principles of this kingdom are gentleness, love, and coherence–all supported by hard work. Also, the bee-like children are asked to understand and measure everything linearly, in terms of endings, judgment, death. The Darwinian crocodile, however, is simply there, outside of time, order, and sentimentality. Wonderland pressures expose adult, above-ground ordering structures as vicious lies.

But Alice, here and elsewhere, very much wants those lies. She is unable to comprehend a world where things do not end–"It's always tea-time!"–, where there are no predatory systems, where logical causality does not hold–"They never executes nobody, you know"–, where, finally, "*Everybody* has won, and *all* must have prizes." Alice seems unable to abandon habits of mind based on logical ordering and linear completion. She insists on progress–"I thought of the future, whatever I did"–a structure which leads her straight to the trial scene, a central parody of above-ground lunacy. Significantly, she finds herself most at home in a courtroom, the epitome of the above-ground passion for ordering, for imagining that everything, even death, is under reasonable control, that only the guilty and the bad die and that we, the virtuous, can ward off all that with our systems. Most centrally, she needs to imagine that the world is significant, full of meanings. Like the Duchess, she believes "Everything's got a moral, if only you can find it." Alice's search for meaning is endless. When she finds nothing, she does not reject her postulate; she simply rejects the entire adventure and the implications of her dream: "You're nothing but a pack of cards!" She is understandably resistant to the terrors of anarchy. Ironically, she is also resistant to the liberation that anarchy offers, unable to enter into a world of free-play. She is, in this sense, ineducable.

She is, at heart, resistant to childhood as it is imaged in this work. Unhappily, she carries with her the destructive adult perceptions the book is so busy attacking. She is, thus, a mini-adult, treated ambiguously, alternately fawned over and hacked at. Alice is both a loving "dream-child" and a "serpent."

I do not mean to suggest that Carroll had it in for Alice Liddell in particular. He later said that the Alice in the book was "my dream-child," a phrase that can be taken to indicate that the fictional Alice is some composite of child-friends, partly idealized but also resented, insofar as she is strangely reluctant to play out the wish-fulfillment dream. She reenacts, by growing up, the pattern of commitment and abandonment experienced by Carroll over and over with little girls. Just as Alice refuses to succumb to the lure of Wonderland and abruptly leaves it, so did almost all of the child-friends eventually drift away from the extraordinary play and affection offered to them by Carroll.

The story of Carroll's love for little girls – and his detestation of boys: "I think they are a mistake" – is well-known. Armed with safety pins to fasten skirts for wading and with various attractive games and puzzles, he would find ways to meet children at the sea-side; he sought (with success) acquaintance of parents (of the proper class) with attractive daughters so as to take the children on various excursions, ordinarily to the theatre, entertain them in his rooms at Christ Church, or photograph them in costumes or in the nude. The intensity with which he pursued this love was matched only by his passionate insistence on its innocence. While letters reveal that a few (surprisingly very few) parents found something amiss in these dealings and while there clearly was gossip enough to cause Carroll's sister Mary to express concern, there can be little question but that the dealings with children were technically innocent. There can also be no question but that they were charged with great erotic force. This is not, of course, to suggest that Carroll in any way harmed the children or intruded on them an unaccepted or unreciprocated energy. Rather, there appears to have been a match of sexual needs and forces, as well as considerable gentleness and tenderness. The reminiscences written later by these child-friends suggest, by their warmth and remarkable recall of detail, an experience not only acceptable but joyous and nurturing.

Carroll's own feelings about these affairs were more complex. The pleasure he derived from them is obvious: "Ah, happy he who owns that tendrest joy,/ The heart-love of a child!" The problem was that he could never fully own the joy or the heart-love – at least not for long. As a consequence, there is some inevitable edginess present, even in the correspondence. Carroll is constantly hectoring his child-friends about their forms of epistolary closing, chiding them with uneasy jokes when any slip from "Yours affectionately" (or better, "Your loving") is noted. And all *are* noted. A diary entry records the receipt of two notes from girls: "Both begin 'my dear' (instead of 'dearest') and are 'affectionate' (instead of ('loving'). The love of children is a fleeting thing." He could, in fact, become bitterly cynical about his predictably disloyal friends: "Sorrowful experience has taught me that the affection of most *children* is in exact proportion to the amount of pleasure they receive, or expect, from anybody: it is in fact identical with self-interest."

Calculation and dissimulation were, however, minor problems in comparison with the truly destructive characteristic of these children: their insistence on growing up: "About 9 out of 10, I think, of my child-friendships get shipwrecked at the critical point 'where the stream and river meet'." He perceives the natural process of growth as distinctly unnatural, a rejection of freedom and play and a nearly idiotic acceptance of the world of the governesses. More pointedly, it is a rejection of Carroll and the love he is so eager to give.

Alice in Wonderland is, from this point of view, a special and seductive invitation to the dream-Alice to remain a child, to stay within the magic circle Carroll created and then lost with virtually every child he knew. The work ends with the wistful and poignant hope that Alice will retain through her adult years "the simple and loving heart of her childhood," a heart fixed with Carroll. Like the commercials that remind us of time's swift flight and advise us to freeze our children in film before it is too late, this book reveals a desire for a marble-like stasis. But there is also present a recognition, often expressed in self-pitying or angry terms, that the child will grow – will grow *away* – and that, as the prefatory poem to *Through the Looking-Glass* says so bluntly, "No thought of me shall find a place / In thy young life's hereafter."

Alice, sadly, is never really tempted to accept the Wonderland invitation. For her it is all only an adventure that passes without consequence. She moves with disastrous ease into the prison-house of adulthood, abandoning her old, tender lover. Unhappy, even bitter, but retaining nonetheless the gentleness and the after-traces of love, Carroll is left with a memory only, a dream inhabited by a dream-child. As Carroll knew all too well, the child will wake and run off. Only he remained – and remained faithful to the melancholy, glorious dream.

JAMES R. KINCAID.
Boulder, Colorado, June, 1981.

CHRISTMAS-GREETINGS

[FROM A FAIRY TO A CHILD.]

LADY dear, if Fairies may
For a moment lay aside
Cunning tricks and elfish play,
'Tis at happy Christmas-tide.

We have heard the children say—
Gentle children, whom we love—
Long ago, on Christmas-Day,
Came a message from above.

Still, as Christmas-tide comes round,
They remember it again—
Echo still the joyful sound
"Peace on earth, good-will to men!"

Yet the hearts must child-like be
Where such heavenly guests abide;
Unto children, in their glee,
All the year is Christmas-tide!

Thus, forgetting tricks and play
For a moment, Lady dear,
We would wish you, if we may,
Merry Christmas, glad New Year!

LEWIS CARROLL.
Christmas, 1867.

To All Child-Readers of

ALICE'S ADVENTURES IN WONDERLAND

DEAR CHILDREN,

At Christmas time a few grave words are not quite out of place, I hope, even at the end of a book of nonsense—and I want to take this opportunity of thanking the thousands of children who have read "Alice's Adventures in Wonderland," for the kindly interest they have taken in my little dream-child.

The thought of the many English firesides where happy faces have smiled her a welcome, and of the many English children to whom she has brought an hour of (I trust) innocent amusement, is one of the brightest and pleasantest thoughts of my life. I have a host of young friends already, whose names and whose faces I know—but I cannot help feeling as if, through "Alice's Adventures," I had made friends with many many other dear children, whose faces I shall never see.

To all my little friends, known and unknown, I wish with all my heart, "A Merry Christmas and a Happy New Year." May God bless you, dear children, and make each Christmas-tide, as it comes round to you, more bright and beautiful than the last—bright with the presence of that unseen Friend, Who once on earth blessed little children—and beautiful with memories of a loving life, which has sought and found that truest kind of happiness, the only kind that is really worth the having, the happiness of making others happy too!

Your affectionate friend,
LEWIS CARROLL.
Christmas, 1871.

An Easter Greeting

To Every Child Who Loves

ALICE

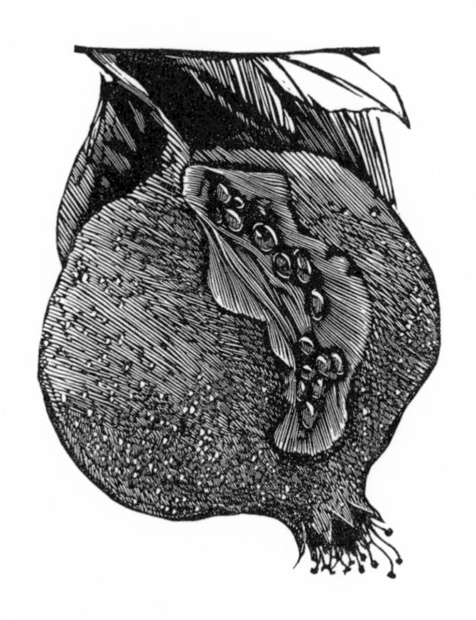

MY DEAR CHILD,

Please to fancy, if you can, that you are reading a real letter, from a real friend whom you have seen, and whose voice you can seem to yourself to hear, wishing you, as I do now with all my heart, a happy Easter.

Do you know that delicious dreamy feeling, when one first wakes on a summer morning, with the twitter of birds in the air, and the fresh breeze coming in at the open window—when, lying lazily with eyes half shut, one sees as in a dream green boughs waving, or waters rippling in a golden light? It is a pleasure very near to sadness, bringing tears to one's eyes like a beautiful picture or poem. And is not that a Mother's gentle hand that undraws your curtains, and a Mother's sweet voice that summons you to rise? To rise and forget, in the bright sunlight, the ugly dreams that frightened you so when all was dark—to rise and enjoy another happy day, first kneeling to thank that unseen Friend who sends you the beautiful sun?

Are these strange words from a writer of such tales as "Alice"? And is this a strange letter to find in a book of nonsense? It may be so. Some perhaps may blame me for thus mixing together things grave and gay; others may smile and think it odd that any one should speak of solemn things at all, except in Church and on a Sunday: but I think—nay, I am sure—that some children will read this gently and lovingly, and in the spirit in which I have written it.

For I do not believe God means us thus to divide life into two halves—to wear a grave face on Sunday, and to think it out-of-place to even so much as mention Him on a week-day. Do you think He cares to see only kneeling figures and to hear only tones of prayer—and that He does not also love to see the lambs leaping in the sunlight, and to hear the merry voices of the children, as they roll among the hay? Surely their innocent laughter is as sweet in His ears as the grandest anthem that ever rolled up from the "dim religious light" of some solemn cathedral?

And if I have written anything to add to those stores of innocent and healthy amusement that are laid up in books for the children I love so well, it is surely something I may hope to look back upon without shame and sorrow (as how much of life must then be recalled!) when *my* turn comes to walk through the valley of shadows.

This Easter sun will rise on you, dear child, feeling your "life in every limb," and eager to rush out into the fresh morning air—and many an Easter-day will come and go, before it finds you feeble and grey-headed, creeping wearily out to bask once more in the sunlight—but it is good, even now, to think sometimes of that great morning when "the Sun of righteousness" shall "arise with healing in his wings."

Surely your gladness need not be the less for the thought that you will one day see a brighter dawn than this—when lovelier sights will meet your eyes than any waving trees or rippling waters—when angel-hands shall undraw your curtains, and sweeter tones than ever loving Mother breathed shall wake you to a new and glorious day—and when all the sadness, and the sin, that darkened life on this little earth, shall be forgotten like the dreams of a night that is past!

Your affectionate friend,
LEWIS CARROLL.
Easter, 1876.

Preface to the

EIGHTY-SIXTH THOUSAND

of the 6/- Edition.

Enquiries have been so often addressed to me, as to whether any answer to the Hatter's Riddle (see p.97) [p.83 in this edition] can be imagined, that I may as well put on record here what seems to me to be a fairly appropriate answer, viz. "Because it can produce a few notes, though they are *very* flat; and it is nevar put with the wrong end in front!" This, however, is merely an after-thought: the Riddle, as originally invented, had no answer at all.

For this eighty-sixth thousand, fresh electrotypes have been taken from the wood-blocks (which, never having been used for printing from, are in as good condition as when first cut in 1865), and the whole book has been set up afresh with new type. If the artistic qualities of this re-issue fall short, in any particular, of those possessed by the original issue, it will not be for want of painstaking on the part of author, publisher, or printer.

I take this opportunity of announcing that the Nursery "Alice," hitherto priced at four shillings, net, is now to be had on the same terms as the ordinary shilling picture-books—although I feel sure that it is, in every quality (except the *text* itself, on which I am not qualified to pronounce), greatly superior to them. Four shillings was a perfectly reasonable price to charge, considering the very heavy initial outlay I had incurred: still, as the Public have practically said "We will *not* give more than a shilling for a picture-book, however artistically got-up", I am content to reckon my outlay on the book as so much dead loss, and, rather than let the little ones, for whom it was written, go without it, I am selling it at a price which is, to me, much the same thing as *giving* it away.

Christmas, 1896.

ALICE'S ADVENTURES IN WONDERLAND

"ALL IN THE GOLDEN AFTERNOON..."

All in the golden afternoon
Full leisurely we glide;
For both our oars, with little skill,
By little arms are plied,
While little hands make vain pretence
Our wanderings to guide.

Ah, cruel Three! In such an hour,
Beneath such dreamy weather,
To beg a tale of breath too weak
To stir the tiniest feather!
Yet what can one poor voice avail
Against three tongues together?

Imperious Prima flashes forth
Her edict "to begin it":
In gentler tones Secunda hopes
"There will be nonsense in it!"
While Tertia interrupts the tale
Not more *than once a minute.*

Anon, to sudden silence won,
In fancy they pursue
The dream-child moving through a land
Of wonders wild and new,
In friendly chat with bird or beast—
And half believe it true.

And ever, as the story drained
The wells of fancy dry,
And faintly strove that weary one
To put the subject by,
"The rest next time—" "It is *next time!"*
The happy voices cry.

To pass the time on a rowing expedition from Folly Bridge to Godstow on July 4, 1862, Carroll began a story, plopping 'my heroine straight down a rabbit-hole, to begin with, without the least idea what was to happen afterwards.' Present on the occasion were the three daughters of Dean Liddell – Lorina ('Prima'), Alice ('Secunda'), and Edith ('Tertia') – and the Reverend Robinson Duckworth, then a fellow of Trinity. Later, 'to please a child I loved,' Carroll wrote out the story, the original version of ALICE'S ADVENTURES IN WONDERLAND, *called* ALICE'S ADVENTURES UNDER GROUND. *Though the Meteorological Office records indicate that a good deal of rain fell in the twelve hours prior to 2 a.m. on July 5, Duckworth, Dodgson, and Alice each remembered the day as sunny and warm. Their recollections are expertly supported and the confusion cleared up by H. B. Doherty in an essay in* WEATHER *(1968). We can now be assured that it indeed was warm and sunny, a 'golden afternoon.'*

Thus grew the tale of Wonderland:
Thus slowly, one by one,
Its quaint events were hammered out—
And now the tale is done,
And home we steer, a merry crew,
Beneath the setting sun.

Alice! A childish story take,
And, with a gentle hand,
Lay it where Childhood's dreams are twined
In Memory's mystic band,
Like pilgrim's wither'd wreath of flowers
Pluck'd in a far-off land.

Down the Rabbit-Hole

ALICE WAS BEGINNING TO GET very tired of sitting by her sister on the bank, and of having nothing to do: once or twice she had peeped into the book her sister was reading, but it had no pictures or conversations in it, "and what is the use of a book," thought Alice, "without pictures or conversations?"

So she was considering, in her own mind (as well as she could, for the hot day made her feel very sleepy and stupid), whether the pleasure of making a daisy-chain would be worth the trouble of getting up and picking the daisies, when suddenly a White Rabbit with pink eyes ran close by her.

There was nothing so *very* remarkable in that; nor did Alice think it so *very* much out of the way to hear the Rabbit say to himself "Oh dear! Oh dear! I shall be too late!" (when she thought it over afterwards, it occurred to her that she ought to have wondered at this, but at the time it all seemed quite natural); but, when the Rabbit actually *took a watch out of his waistcoat-pocket,* and looked at it, and then hurried on, Alice started to her feet, for it flashed across her mind that she had never before seen a rabbit with either a waistcoat-pocket, or a watch to take out of it, and, burning with curiosity,[2] she ran across the field after him, and fortunately was just in time to see him pop down a large rabbit-hole under the hedge.

In another moment down went Alice after him, never once considering how in the world she was to get out again.

The rabbit-hole went straight on like a tunnel for some way, and then dipped suddenly down, so suddenly that Alice had not a moment to think about stopping herself before she found herself falling down a very deep well.

2 *The fact that this term is used so often and with such positive associations indicates something about Carroll's militant anti-didacticism and the more liberal cultural attitudes toward children's literature prevalent by the mid-60's. Earlier, curiosity had commonly been viewed as an alarming characteristic, one that should be stamped out by all vigorous measures.* A PUZZLE FOR A CURIOUS GIRL *(1802), for instance, recounts a witless puzzle, the clue to which is the damage done by curious children. The elaborately undisguised moral is: 'Do not suppose that curiosity is such a trifle, as to stand in no need of being combated by divine grace. Nothing is a trifle which leads the way to vice.' The cure advocated—'a habit of constant employment'—is the same advanced by the Isaac Watts poem parodied a few pages later. For a fascinating historical account of theological and secular attitudes toward curiosity see Christian Zacher's* CURIOSITY AND PILGRIMAGE *(Johns Hopkins, 1976).*

Either the well was very deep, or she fell very slowly, for she had plenty of time as she went down to look about her, and to wonder what was going to happen next. First, she tried to look down and

make out what she was coming to, but it was too dark to see anything: then she looked at the sides of the well, and noticed that they were filled with cupboards and book-shelves: here and there she saw maps and pictures hung upon pegs. She took down a jar from one of the shelves as she passed: it was labeled "ORANGE MARMALADE," but to her great disappointment it was empty: she did not like to drop the jar, for fear of killing somebody,[3] so managed to put it into one of the cupboards as she fell past it.

"Well!" thought Alice to herself. "After such a fall as this, I shall think nothing of tumbling down-stairs! How brave they'll all think me at home! Why, I wouldn't say anything about it, even if I fell off the top of the house!" (Which was very likely true.)[4]

Down, down, down. Would the fall *never* come to an end? "I wonder how many miles I've fallen by this time?" she said aloud. "I must be getting somewhere near the centre of the earth. Let me see: that would be four thousand miles down, I think—" (for, you see, Alice had learnt several things of this sort in her lessons in the school-room, and though this was not a *very* good opportunity for showing off her knowledge, as there was no one to listen to her, still it was good practice to say it over) "—yes, that's about the right distance—but then I wonder what Latitude or Longitude I've got to?" (Alice had no idea what Latitude was, or Longitude either, but thought they were nice grand words to say.)

Presently she began again. "I wonder if I shall fall right *through* the earth! How funny it'll seem to come out among the people that walk with their heads downwards! The antipathies, I think—" (she was rather glad there *was* no one listening, this time, as it didn't sound at all the right word) "—but I shall have to ask them what the name of the country is, you know. Please, Ma'am, is this New Zealand? Or Australia?" (and she tried to curtsey as she spoke—fancy, *curtseying* as you're falling through the air! Do you think you could manage it?) "And what an ignorant little girl she'll think me! No, it'll never do to ask: perhaps I shall see it written up somewhere."

Down, down, down. There was nothing else to do, so Alice soon began talking again. "Dinah'll miss me very much to-night, I should think!" (Dinah was the cat.)[5] "I hope they'll remember her saucer of milk at tea-time. Dinah, my dear! I wish you were down here with me! There are no mice in the air, I'm afraid, but you might catch a bat, and that's very like a mouse, you know. But do cats eat bats, I wonder?" And here Alice began to get rather sleepy, and went on saying to herself, in a dreamy sort of way, "Do cats eat bats? Do cats eat bats?" and sometimes "Do bats eat cats?", for, you see, as she couldn't answer either question, it didn't much matter which way she put it.[6] She felt that she was dozing off, and

3 This is the first of a surprising number of references to death. The prominence of death, particularly as it is understood by Alice, is suggestive of one adult ordering system: death appears as the consequence of insisting on linear developments, endings.

4 This is the first (and one of the grimmest) of many jokes which work by taking idiomatic phrases literally. The letters to child-friends are full of such play: 'Boo! hoo! Here's Mr. Dodgson has drunk my health, and I haven't got any left!' The effect of these puns is to unfreeze language and to reveal its instability. Even the simplest terms refuse to stay put, as Carroll observed in a letter to Alice: 'I crossed out most because it's ambiguous; most words are, I fear.'

5 The Liddell children's tabby cat was named Dinah.

6 Alice's above-ground understanding of the order of things depends greatly on predation: who eats whom. On the whole, Wonderland appears to have no such system.

had just begun to dream that she was walking hand in hand with Dinah, and saying to her, very earnestly, "Now, Dinah, tell me the truth: did you ever eat a bat?" when suddenly, thump! thump! down she came upon a heap of dry leaves, and the fall was over.

Alice was not a bit hurt, and she jumped up on to her feet in a moment: she looked up, but it was all dark overhead: before her was another long passage, and the White Rabbit was still in sight, hurrying down it. There was not a moment to be lost: away went Alice like the wind, and was just in time to hear him say, as he turned a corner, "Oh my ears and whiskers, how late it's getting!" She was close behind him when she turned the corner, but the Rabbit was no longer to be seen: she found herself in a long, low hall, which was lit up by a row of lamps hanging from the roof.

There were doors all round the hall, but they were all locked; and when Alice had been all the way down one side and up the other, trying every door, she walked sadly down the middle, wondering how she was ever to get out again.

Suddenly she came upon a little three-legged table, all made of solid glass: there was nothing on it except a tiny golden key, and Alice's first thought was that it might belong to one of the doors of the hall; but, alas! Either the locks were too large, or the key was too small, but at any rate it would not open any of them. However, the second time round, she came upon a low curtain she had not noticed before, and behind it was a little door about fifteen inches high: she tried the little golden key in the lock, and to her great delight it fitted!

Alice opened the door and found that it led into a small passage, not much larger than a rat-hole: she knelt down and looked along the passage into the loveliest garden you ever saw. How she longed to get out of that dark hall, and wander about among those beds of bright flowers and those cool fountains, but she could not even get her head through the doorway; "and even if my head *would* go through," thought poor Alice, "it would be of very little use without my shoulders. Oh, how I wish I could shut up like a telescope! I think I could, if I only knew how to begin." For, you see, so many out-of-the-way things had happened lately, that Alice had begun to think that very few things indeed were really impossible.

There seemed to be no use in waiting by the little door, so she went back to the table, half hoping she might find another key on it, or at any rate a book of rules for shutting people up like telescopes: this time she found a little bottle on it ("which certainly was not here before," said Alice), and round its neck a paper label, with the words "DRINK ME" beautifully printed on it in large letters.

It was all very well to say "Drink me," but the wise little Alice was not going to do *that* in a hurry. "No, I'll look first," she said, "and see whether it's marked '*poison*' or not"; for she had read several nice little histories about children who had got burnt, and eaten up by wild beasts, and many other unpleasant things, all because they *would* not remember the simple rules their friends had taught them:[7] such as, that a red-hot poker will burn you if you hold it too long; and that, if you cut your finger *very* deeply with a knife, it usually bleeds;[8] and she had never forgotten that, if you drink much from a bottle marked "*poison*," it is almost certain to disagree with you, sooner or later.

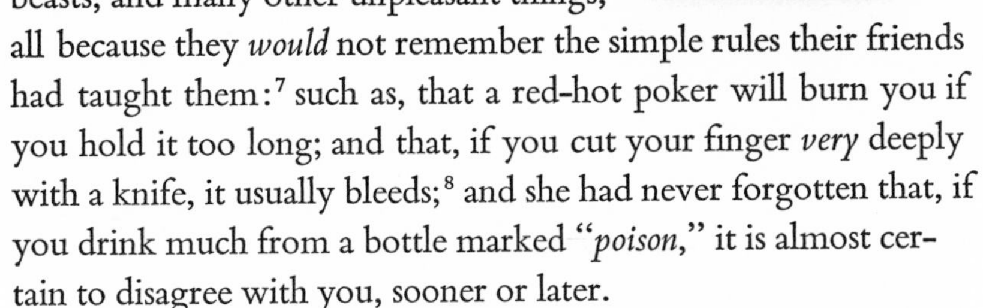

However, this bottle was *not* marked "*poison*," so Alice ventured to taste it, and, finding it very nice (it had, in fact, a sort of mixed flavour of cherry-tart, custard, pine-apple, roast turkey, toffy, and hot buttered toast), she very soon finished it off.

* * * * * * * * * * [9]

"What a curious feeling!" said Alice. "I must be shutting up like a telescope!"

And so it was indeed: she was now only ten inches high, and her face brightened up at the thought that she was now the right size for going through the little door into that lovely garden. First, however, she waited for a few minutes to see if she was going to shrink any further: she felt a little nervous about this; "for it might end, you know," said Alice, "in my going out altogether, like a candle. I wonder what I should be like then?"[10] And she tried to fancy what the flame of a candle is like after it is blown out, for she could not remember ever having seen such a thing.

After a while, finding that nothing more happened, she decided on going into the garden at once; but, alas for poor Alice! When she got to the door, she found she had forgotten the little golden key, and when she went back to the table for it, she found she could not possibly reach it: she could see it quite plainly through the glass, and she tried her best to climb up one of the table-legs,

7 The plots here offer mild exaggerations of a moralistic, cautionary children's literature that reflects an attitude toward children and life consistently subverted by Carroll. He was very proud of the fact that ALICE *was free of such didacticism, writing to his niece, to whom he was sending a gift, 'The book has got a moral—so I need hardly say it is* NOT *by Lewis Carroll.'*

8 An amusing variation of this theme occurs in a letter to a child-friend: 'Whenever you wish to punish your brothers, you will find it very convenient to do so by running the knife into their hands and faces (particularly the end of the nose); you will find it gives a good deal of pain if you run it in hard enough.'

9 Carroll used these asterisks, not very consistently, to mark abrupt changes in Alice's size. In this edition all twelve size changes are indicated by either red (original) or blue (interpolated) asterisks.

10 This simile is repeated more vigorously and threateningly by Tweedledum in THROUGH THE LOOKING-GLASS: *'If that there King was to wake, . . . you'd go out—bang!—just like a candle!'*

but it was too slippery; and when she had tired herself out with trying, the poor little thing sat down and cried.

"Come, there's no use in crying like that!" said Alice to herself rather sharply. "I advise you to leave off this minute!" She generally gave herself very good advice (though she very seldom followed it), and sometimes she scolded herself so severely as to bring tears into her eyes; and once she remembered trying to box her own ears for having cheated herself in a game of croquet she was playing against herself, for this curious child was very fond of pretending to be two people. "But it's no use now," thought poor Alice, "to pretend to be two people! Why, there's hardly enough of me left to make *one* respectable person!"

Soon her eye fell on a little glass box that was lying under the table: she opened it, and found in it a very small cake, on which the words "EAT ME" were beautifully marked in currants. "Well, I'll eat it," said Alice, "and if it makes me larger, I can reach the key; and if it makes me smaller, I can creep under the door: so either way I'll get into the garden, and I don't care which happens!"

She ate a little bit, and said anxiously to herself "Which way? Which way?", holding her hand on the top of her head to feel which way it was growing; and she was quite surprised to find that she remained the same size. To be sure, this generally happens when one eats cake; but Alice had got so much into the way of expecting nothing but out-of-the-way things to happen, that it seemed quite dull and stupid for life to go on in the common way.

So she set to work, and very soon finished off the cake.

* * * * * * * * * * *

II

The Pool of Tears

"Curiouser and curiouser!" cried Alice (she was so much surprised, that for the moment she quite forgot how to speak good English).[11] "Now I'm opening out like the largest telescope that ever was! Good-bye, feet!" (for when she looked down at her feet, they seemed to be almost out of sight, they were getting so far off). "Oh, my poor little feet, I wonder who will put on your shoes and stockings for you now, dears? I'm sure *I* sha'n't be able! I shall be a great deal too far off to trouble myself about you: you must manage the best way you can—but I must be kind to them," thought Alice, "or perhaps they wo'n't walk the way I want to go! Let me see. I'll give them a new pair of boots every Christmas."

And she went on planning to herself how she would manage it. "They must go by the carrier," she thought; "and how funny it'll seem, sending presents to one's own feet! And how odd the directions will look!

Alice's Right Foot, Esq.,
Hearthrug,
near the Fender,[12]
(with Alice's love).

Oh dear, what nonsense I'm talking!"

Just at this moment her head struck against the roof of the hall: in fact she was now rather more than nine feet high, and she at once took up the little golden key and hurried off to the garden door.

Poor Alice! It was as much as she could do, lying down on one side, to look through into the garden with one eye; but to get through was more hopeless than ever: she sat down and began to cry again.

11 *The notion that 'good English' has a natural existence as a cultural tool one can master is exploded by a hundred hidden mines in this book (and more explicitly in* THROUGH THE LOOKING-GLASS *by Humpty Dumpty). Language is certainly not figured as our servant, nor even as a trustworthy friend. Interestingly, Dodgson was capable of exercising his characteristic fussiness on this point, lecturing his sister on her errors and blaming the newspapers 'for the bad English' now rampant, particularly in novels: 'How few novels of the day are written in correct English!'*

12 *A fender is a metal frame, often highly ornamented, designed to keep fireplace coals from rolling into the room.*

"You ought to be ashamed of yourself," said Alice, "a great girl like you," (she might well say this), "to go on crying in this way! Stop this moment, I tell you!" But she went on all the same, shedding gallons of tears, until there was a large pool all round her, about four inches deep, and reaching half down the hall.

After a time she heard a little pattering of feet in the distance, and she hastily dried her eyes to see what was coming. It was the White Rabbit returning, splendidly dressed, with a pair of white kid-gloves in one hand and a large fan in the other: he came trotting along in a great hurry, muttering to himself, as he came, "Oh! The Duchess, the Duchess! Oh! *Wo'n't* she be savage if I've kept her waiting!" Alice felt so desperate that she was ready to ask help of any one: so, when the Rabbit came near her, she began, in a low, timid voice, "If you please, Sir—" The Rabbit started violently, dropped the white kid-gloves and the fan, and scurried away into the darkness as hard as he could go.

Alice took up the fan and gloves, and, as the hall was very hot, she kept fanning herself all the time she went on talking. "Dear, dear! How queer everything is to-day! And yesterday things went on just as usual. I wonder if I've been changed in the night? Let me think: *was I* the same when I got up this morning? I almost think I can remember feeling a little different. But if I'm not the same, the next question is 'Who in the world am I?' Ah, *that's* the great puzzle!" And she began thinking over all the children she knew that were of the same age as herself, to see if she could have been changed for any of them.

"I'm sure I'm not Ada," she said, "for her hair goes in such long ringlets, and mine doesn't go in ringlets at all; and I'm sure I ca'n't be Mabel, for I know all sorts of things, and she, oh, she knows such a very little! Besides, *she's* she, and *I'm* I, and—oh dear, how puzzling it all is! I'll try if I know all the things I used to know. Let me see: four times five is twelve, and four times six is thirteen, and four times seven is—oh dear! I shall never get to twenty at that rate![13] However, the Multiplication-Table doesn't signify: let's try Geography. London is the capital of Paris, and Paris is the capital of Rome, and Rome—no, *that's* all wrong, I'm certain! I must have been changed for Mabel! I'll try and say *'How doth the little—',*" and she crossed her hands on her lap, as if she were saying lessons, and began to repeat it, but her voice sounded hoarse and strange, and the words did not come the same as they used to do:—

"How doth the little crocodile
Improve his shining tail,
And pour the waters of the Nile
On every golden scale!

"How cheerfully he seems to grin,
How neatly spreads his claws,
And welcomes little fishes in,
With gently smiling jaws![14]

"I'm sure those are not the right words," said poor Alice, and her eyes filled with tears again as she went on, "I must be Mabel after all, and I shall have to go and live in that poky little house, and have next to no toys to play with,[15] and oh, ever so many lessons to learn! No, I've made up my mind about it: if I'm Mabel, I'll stay down here! It'll be no use their putting their heads down and saying 'Come up again, dear!' I shall only look up and say 'Who am I, then? Tell me that first, and then, if I like being that person, I'll come up: if not, I'll stay down here till I'm somebody else' —but, oh dear!" cried Alice, with a sudden burst of tears, "I do wish they *would* put their heads down! I am so *very* tired of being all alone here!"

* * * * * * * * * * *

As she said this she looked down at her hands, and was surprised to see that she had put on one of the Rabbit's little white kid-gloves while she was talking. "How *can* I have done that?" she thought. "I must be growing small again." She got up and went to the table to measure herself by it, and found that, as nearly as she could

13 Many explanations, based on different numerical scales, have been offered. The simplest, based on scale 10, is given by Martin Gardner in THE ANNOTATED ALICE. *He argues that since 'the multiplication table traditionally stops with the twelves, . . . if you continue this nonsense progression – 4 times 5 is 12, 4 times 6 is 13, 4 times 7 is 14, and so on – you end with 4 times 12 . . . is 19.' Given Dodgson's profession and his interest in complicated puzzles, however, it seems likely that a more sophisticated game is under way. Alexander L. Taylor's proposal (in* THE WHITE KNIGHT*) of an advancing numerical scale is quite convincing. In a letter commenting on the traditional paradox of Achilles and the Tortoise, according to which Achilles can never catch up to the Tortoise, Carroll observed, 'A thing is not* IMPOSSIBLE, *merely because it is* INCONCEIVABLE. *The human reason has very definite limits.'*

14 This parodies Isaac Watts's 'Against Idleness and Mischief,' one of the poems from his DIVINE SONGS FOR CHILDREN *(1715):*

How doth the little busy bee
Improve each shining hour;
And gather honey all the day,
From ev'ry opening flow'r.

How skilfully she builds her cell,
How neat she spreads the wax;
And labours hard to store it well,
With the sweet food she makes.

In works of labour, or of skill,
I would be busy too;
For Satan finds some mischief still,
For idle hands to do.

In books, or work, or healthful play,
Let my first years be past;
That I may give for ev'ry day
Some good account at last.

15 Here and in a few later occurrences, snobbery and an alertness to class distinctions poke through. Dodgson was very

guess, she was now about two feet high, and was going on shrinking rapidly: she soon found out that the cause of this was the fan she was holding, and she dropped it hastily, just in time to save herself from shrinking away altogether.

"That *was* a narrow escape!" said Alice, a good deal frightened at the sudden change, but very glad to find herself still in existence. "And now for the garden!" And she ran with all speed back to the little door; but, alas! The little door was shut again, and the little golden key was lying on the glass table as before, "and things are worse than ever," thought the poor child, "for I never was so small as this before, never! And I declare it's too bad, that it is!"

As she said these words her foot slipped, and in another moment, splash! She was up to her chin in salt-water. Her first idea was that she had somehow fallen into the sea, "and in that case I can go back by railway," she said to herself. (Alice had been to the seaside once in her life, and had come to the general conclusion that, wherever you go to on the English coast, you find a number of bathing-machines[16] in the sea, some children digging in the sand with wooden spades, then a row of lodging-houses, and behind them a railway station.) However, she soon made out that she was in the pool of tears which she had wept when she was nine feet high.

"I wish I hadn't cried so much!" said Alice, as she swam about, trying to find her way out. "I shall be punished for it now, I suppose, by being drowned in my own tears! That *will* be a queer thing, to be sure! However, everything is queer to-day."

Just then she heard something splashing about in the pool a little

particular in his choice of friends, especially his child-friends: 'The children on the beach are not the right sort, YET. *They* ARE *a vulgar-looking lot! I should think there's hardly anyone here, yet, above the "small shop-keeper" rank.' And that was decidedly not the rank he had in mind as an audience for* ALICE: *'My own idea is, that it isn't a book* POOR *children would much care for.'*

16 *Bathing-machines were remarkable contraptions, designed for ensuring privacy while bathing in the sea. They were portable enclosures, rather like circular shower curtains, made to be wheeled into the water. Carroll found them hilarious, often joking about them in letters to child-friends. To one who inquired about the meaning of the Snark, said to be identifiable by 'its fondness for bathing-machines,' he wrote: 'When the people get weary of life, and can't find happiness in town or in books, then they rush off to the seaside, to see what bathing-machines will do for them.'*

way off, and she swam nearer to make out what it was: at first she thought it must be a walrus or hippopotamus, but then she remembered how small she was now, and she soon made out that it was only a mouse, that had slipped in like herself.

"Would it be of any use, now," thought Alice, "to speak to this mouse? Everything is so out-of-the-way down here, that I should think very likely it can talk: at any rate, there's no harm in trying." So she began: "O Mouse, do you know the way out of this pool? I am very tired of swimming about here, O Mouse!" (Alice thought this must be the right way of speaking to a mouse: she had never done such a thing before, but she remembered having seen, in her brother's Latin Grammar, "A mouse—of a mouse—to a mouse—a mouse—O mouse!")[17] The mouse looked at her rather inquisitively, and seemed to her to wink with one of its little eyes, but it said nothing.

17 Selwyn H. Goodacre has identified the source as THE COMIC LATIN GRAMMAR *(1840). This curious book, authored by Percival Leigh, a writer for* PUNCH, *thought to make the study of Latin an occasion for jollity.*

"Perhaps it doesn't understand English," thought Alice. "I daresay it's a French mouse, come over with William the Conqueror." (For, with all her knowledge of history, Alice had no very clear notion how long ago anything had happened.) So she began again: "Où est ma chatte?", which was the first sentence in her French lesson-book.[18] The Mouse gave a sudden leap out of the water, and seemed to quiver all over with fright. "Oh, I beg your pardon!" cried Alice hastily, afraid that she had hurt the poor animal's feelings. "I quite forgot you didn't like cats."

18 The French lesson-book is LA BAGATELLE *(1804). Hugh O'Brien, who first located the source* (NOTES & QUERIES, *1963), argues that the book played an important role in the genesis of* ALICE, *suggesting, among other things, the frantic* W. RABBIT.

"Not like cats!" cried the Mouse in a shrill, passionate voice. "Would *you* like cats, if you were me?"

"Well, perhaps not," said Alice in a soothing tone: "don't be angry about it. And yet I wish I could show you our cat Dinah. I think you'd take a fancy to cats, if you could only see her. She is such a dear quiet thing," Alice went on, half to herself, as she swam lazily about in the pool, "and she sits purring so nicely by the fire, licking her paws and washing her face—and she is such a nice soft thing to nurse—and she's such a capital one for catching mice—oh, I beg your pardon!" cried Alice again, for this time the Mouse was bristling all over, and she felt certain it must be really offended. "We wo'n't talk about her any more, if you'd rather not."

"We, indeed!" cried the Mouse, who was trembling down to the end of its tail. "As if *I* would talk on such a subject! Our family always *hated* cats: nasty, low, vulgar things! Don't let me hear the name again!"

"I wo'n't indeed!" said Alice, in a great hurry to change the subject of conversation. "Are you—are you fond—of—of dogs?" The Mouse did not answer, so Alice went on eagerly: "There is such a nice little dog, near our house, I should like to show you! A little bright-eyed terrier, you know, with oh, such long curly brown hair! And it'll fetch things when you throw them, and it'll sit up and beg for its dinner, and all sorts of things—I ca'n't remember half of them—and it belongs to a farmer, you know, and he says it's so useful, it's worth a hundred pounds! He says it kills all the rats and—oh dear!" cried Alice in a sorrowful tone. "I'm afraid I've offended it again!" For the Mouse was swimming away from her as hard as it could go, and making quite a commotion in the pool as it went.

So she called softly after it, "Mouse dear! Do come back again, and we wo'n't talk about cats, or dogs either, if you don't like them!" When the Mouse heard this, it turned round and swam slowly back to her; its face was quite pale (with passion, Alice thought), and it said, in a low trembling voice, "Let us get to the shore, and then I'll tell you my history, and you'll understand why it is I hate cats and dogs."

It was high time to go, for the pool was getting quite crowded with the birds and animals that had fallen into it: there was a Duck and a Dodo, a Lory and an Eaglet,[19] and several other curious creatures. Alice led the way, and the whole party swam to the shore.

19 This is one of the few private jokes remaining from ALICE'S ADVENTURES UNDER GROUND. *The Duck is Duckworth, the Dodo is Dodgson, the Lory (an Australasian parrot with brilliant plumage that feeds on pollen and nectar) is Lorina, and the Eaglet is Edith. The drenching in the pool refers to a rainy expedition undertaken by the same party a few weeks earlier (June 17). On that occasion, the drying of clothes was done by a friendly landlady.*

III

A Caucus-Race and a Long Tale

They were indeed a queer-looking party that assembled on the bank—the birds with draggled feathers, the animals with their fur clinging close to them, and all dripping wet, cross, and uncomfortable.

The first question of course was, how to get dry again: they had a consultation about this, and after a few minutes it seemed quite natural to Alice to find herself talking familiarly with them, as if she had known them all her life. Indeed, she had quite a long argument with the Lory, who at last turned sulky, and would only say "I'm older than you, and must know better." And this Alice would not allow, without knowing how old it was, and, as the Lory positively refused to tell its age, there was no more to be said.

At last the Mouse, who seemed to be a person of some authority among them, called out "Sit down, all of you, and listen to me! *I'll* soon make you dry enough!" They all sat down at once, in a large ring, with the Mouse in the middle. Alice kept her eyes anxiously fixed on it, for she felt sure she would catch a bad cold if she did not get dry very soon.

"Ahem!" said the Mouse with an important air. "Are you all ready? This is the driest thing I know. Silence all round, if you please! 'William the Conqueror, whose cause was favoured by the pope, was soon submitted to by the English, who wanted leaders, and had been of late much accustomed to usurpation and conquest. *Edwin* and *Morcar*, the earls of *Mercia* and *Northumbria*——' "[20]

"Ugh!" said the Lory, with a shiver.

"I beg your pardon!" said the Mouse, frowning, but very politely. "Did you speak?"

"Not I!" said the Lory, hastily.

"I thought you did," said the Mouse. "I proceed. '*Edwin* and

20 The source of this version of unhappily familiar prose is identified by the editor of Dodgson's DIARIES, *Roger Lancelyn Green, as Havilland Chepmell's* SHORT COURSE OF HISTORY *(1862), which is quoted verbatim.*

Morcar, the earls of *Mercia* and *Northumbria*, declared for him; and even *Stigand*, the patriotic archbishop of *Canterbury*, found it advisable——' "

"Found *what*?" said the Duck.

"Found *it*," the Mouse replied rather crossly: "of course you know what 'it' means."

"I know what 'it' means well enough, when *I* find a thing," said the Duck: "it's generally a frog, or a worm. The question is, what did the archbishop find?"

The Mouse did not notice this question, but hurriedly went on, " '—found it advisable to go with Edgar Atheling to meet William and offer him the crown.

William's conduct at first was moderate. But the insolence of his Normans——' How are you getting on now, my dear?" it continued, turning to Alice as it spoke.

"As wet as ever," said Alice in a melancholy tone: "it doesn't seem to dry me at all."

"In that case," said the Dodo solemnly, rising to its feet, "I move that the meeting adjourn, for the immediate adoption of more energetic remedies——"

"Speak English!" said the Eaglet. "I don't know the meaning of half those long words, and, what's more, I don't believe you do either!" And the Eaglet bent down its head to hide a smile: some of the other birds tittered audibly.

"What I was going to say," said the Dodo in an offended tone, "was, that the best thing to get us dry would be a Caucus-race."[21]

"What *is* a Caucus-race?" said Alice; not that she much wanted to know, but the Dodo had paused as if it thought that *somebody* ought to speak, and no one else seemed inclined to say anything.

"Why," said the Dodo, "the best way to explain it is to do it." (And, as you might like to try the thing yourself, some winter-day, I will tell you how the Dodo managed it.)

First it marked out a race-course, in a sort of circle, ("the exact shape doesn't matter," it said), and then all the party were placed along the course, here and there. There was no "One, two, three, and away!", but they began running when they liked, and left off when they liked, so that it was not easy to know when the race was over. However, when they had been running half an hour or so, and were quite dry again, the Dodo suddenly called out "The race is over!", and they all crowded round it, panting, and asking "But who has won?"

21 The term CAUCUS *is of obscure origins, according to the* OED, *but it apparently arose in New England as a reference to private meetings of political parties or interest groups. In England the term referred to political organizations seeking to manage elections. It was always used negatively, and all parties were quick to deny that they had caucuses.*

This question the Dodo could not answer without a great deal of thought, and it stood for a long time with one finger pressed upon its forehead (the position in which you usually see Shakespeare, in the pictures of him), while the rest waited in silence. At last the Dodo said "*Everybody* has won, and *all* must have prizes."

"But who is to give the prizes?" quite a chorus of voices asked.

"Why, *she*, of course," said the Dodo, pointing to Alice with one finger; and the whole party at once crowded round her, calling out, in a confused way, "Prizes! Prizes!"

Alice had no idea what to do, and in despair she put her hand in her pocket, and pulled out a box of comfits[22] (luckily the salt-water had not got into it), and handed them round as prizes. There was exactly one a-piece, all round.

22 Comfits are sweetmeats, such as sugar-plums, made by preserving fruit, nuts, or roots in sugar.

"But she must have a prize herself, you know," said the Mouse.

"Of course," the Dodo replied very gravely. "What else have you got in your pocket?" it went on, turning to Alice.

"Only a thimble," said Alice sadly.

"Hand it over here," said the Dodo.

Then they all crowded round her once more, while the Dodo solemnly presented the thimble, saying "We beg your acceptance of this elegant thimble"; and, when it had finished this short speech, they all cheered.

Alice thought the whole thing very absurd, but they all looked so grave that she did not dare to laugh; and, as she could not think of anything to say, she simply bowed, and took the thimble, looking as solemn as she could.

The next thing was to eat the comfits: this caused some noise and confusion, as the large birds complained that they could not taste theirs, and the small ones choked and had to be patted on the back. However, it was over at last, and they sat down again in a ring, and begged the Mouse to tell them something more.

"You promised to tell me your history, you know," said Alice, "and why it is you hate—C and D," she added in a whisper, half afraid that it would be offended again.

"Mine is a long and sad tale!" said the Mouse, turning to Alice, and sighing.

"It *is* a long tail, certainly," said Alice, looking down with wonder at the Mouse's tail; "but why do you call it sad?" And she kept on puzzling about it while the Mouse was speaking, so that her idea of the tale was something like this:—

"Fury said to a mouse,
That he met in the
house, 'Let us both
go to law: *I* will
prosecute *you.*—
Come, I'll take no
denial: We must
have the trial;
For really this
morning I've
nothing to do.'
Said the mouse
to the cur,
'Such a trial,
dear sir,
With no
jury or
judge,
would
be wast-
ing our
breath.'
'I'll be
judge,
I'll be
jury,'
said
cun-
ning
old
Fury:
'I'll
try
the
whole
cause,
and
con-
demn
you
to
d
e
a
t
h.'"

"You are not attending!" said the Mouse to Alice, severely. "What are you thinking of?"

"I beg your pardon," said Alice very humbly: "you had got to the fifth bend, I think?"

"I had *not*!" cried the Mouse, angrily.

"A knot!" said Alice, always ready to make herself useful, and looking anxiously about her. "Oh, do let me help to undo it!"

"I shall do nothing of the sort," said the Mouse, getting up and walking away. "You insult me by talking such nonsense!"

"I didn't mean it!" pleaded poor Alice. "But you're so easily offended, you know!"

The Mouse only growled in reply.

"Please come back and finish your story!" Alice called after it. And the others all joined in chorus "Yes, please do!" But the Mouse only shook its head impatiently, and walked a little quicker.

"What a pity it wouldn't stay!" sighed the Lory, as soon as it was quite out of sight. And an old Crab took the opportunity of saying to her daughter "Ah, my dear! Let this be a lesson to you never to lose *your* temper!" "Hold your tongue, Ma!" said the young Crab, a little snappishly. "You're enough to try the patience of an oyster!"

"I wish I had our Dinah here, I know I do!" said Alice aloud, addressing nobody in particular. "*She'd* soon fetch it back!"

"And who is Dinah, if I might venture to ask the question?" said the Lory.

Alice replied eagerly, for she was always ready to talk about her pet: "Dinah's our cat. And she's such a capital one for catching mice, you ca'n't think! And oh, I wish you could see her after the birds! Why, she'll eat a little bird as soon as look at it!"

This speech caused a remarkable sensation among the party. Some of the birds hurried off at once: one old Magpie began wrapping itself up very carefully, remarking "I really must be getting home: the night-air doesn't suit my throat!" And a Canary called out in a trembling voice to her children "Come away, my dears! It's high time you were all in bed!" On various pretexts they all moved off, and Alice was soon left alone.

"I wish I hadn't mentioned Dinah!" she said to herself in a melancholy tone. "Nobody seems to like her, down here, and I'm sure she's the best cat in the world! Oh, my dear Dinah! I wonder if I shall ever see you any more!" And here poor Alice began to cry again, for she felt very lonely and low-spirited. In a little while, however, she again heard a little pattering of footsteps in the distance, and she looked up eagerly, half hoping that the Mouse had changed its mind, and was coming back to finish its story.[23]

23 This is a pointed reference to Alice's desire for conclusions. The tale had, after all, ended with the word 'death.'

IV

The Rabbit Sends in a Little Bill

It was the White Rabbit, trotting slowly back again, and looking anxiously about as he went, as if he had lost something; and she heard him muttering to himself "The Duchess! The Duchess! Oh my dear paws! Oh my fur and whiskers! She'll get me executed, as sure as ferrets are ferrets! Where *can* I have dropped them, I wonder?" Alice guessed in a moment that he was looking for the fan and the pair of white kid-gloves, and she very good-naturedly began hunting about for them, but they were nowhere to be seen—everything seemed to have changed since her swim in the pool; and the great hall, with the glass table and the little door, had vanished completely.

Very soon the Rabbit noticed Alice, as she went hunting about, and called out to her, in an angry tone, "Why, Mary Ann, what *are* you doing out here? Run home this moment, and fetch me a pair of gloves and a fan! Quick, now!" And Alice was so much frightened that she ran off at once in the direction he pointed to, without trying to explain the mistake that he had made.

"He took me for his housemaid," she said to herself as she ran. "How surprised he'll be when he finds out who I am! But I'd better take him his fan and gloves—that is, if I can find them." As she said this, she came upon a neat little house, on the door of which was a bright brass plate with the name "W. RABBIT" engraved upon it. She went in without knocking, and hurried upstairs, in great fear lest she should meet the real Mary Ann, and be turned out of the house before she had found the fan and gloves.

"How queer it seems," Alice said to herself, "to be going messages for a rabbit! I suppose Dinah'll be sending me on messages next!" And she began fancying the sort of thing that would happen: " 'Miss Alice! Come here directly, and get ready for your walk!' 'Coming in a minute, nurse! But I've got to watch this mouse-hole till Dinah comes back, and see that the mouse doesn't get out.' Only I don't think," Alice went on, "that they'd let Dinah stop in the house if she began ordering people about like that!"

By this time she had found her way into a tidy little room with a table in the window, and on it (as she had hoped) a fan and two or three pairs of tiny white kid-gloves: she took up the fan and a pair of the gloves, and was just going to leave the room, when her eye fell upon a little bottle that stood near the looking-glass. There

was no label this time with the words "DRINK ME," but nevertheless she uncorked it and put it to her lips. "I know *something* interesting is sure to happen," she said to herself, "whenever I eat or drink anything: so I'll just see what this bottle does. I do hope it'll make me grow large again, for really I'm quite tired of being such a tiny little thing!"

*   *   *   *   *   *   *   *   *   *   *

It did so indeed, and much sooner than she had expected: before she had drunk half the bottle, she found her head pressing against the ceiling, and had to stoop to save her neck from being broken. She hastily put down the bottle, saying to herself "That's quite enough—I hope I sha'n't grow any more—As it is, I ca'n't get out at the door—I do wish I hadn't drunk quite so much!"

Alas! It was too late to wish that! She went on growing, and growing, and very soon had to kneel down on the floor: in another minute there was not even room for this, and she tried the effect of lying down with one elbow against the door, and the other arm curled round her head. Still she went on growing, and, as a last resource, she put one arm out of the window, and one foot up the chimney,[24] and said to herself "Now I can do no more, whatever happens. What *will* become of me?"

Luckily for Alice, the little magic bottle had now had its full effect, and she grew no larger: still it was very uncomfortable, and, as there seemed to be no sort of chance of her ever getting out of the room again, no wonder she felt unhappy.

"It was much pleasanter at home," thought poor Alice, "when one wasn't always growing larger and smaller, and being ordered about by mice and rabbits. I almost wish I hadn't gone down that rabbit-hole—and yet—and yet—it's rather curious, you know, this sort of life! I do wonder what *can* have happened to me! When I used to read fairy tales, I fancied that kind of thing never happened, and now here I am in the middle of one! There ought to be a book written about me, that there ought! And when I grow up, I'll write one—but I'm grown up now," she added in a sorrowful tone: "at least there's no room to grow up any more *here*."[25]

"But then," thought Alice, "shall I *never* get any older than I am now? That'll be a comfort, one way—never to be an old woman—but then—always to have lessons to learn! Oh, I shouldn't like *that*!"

"Oh, you foolish Alice!" she answered herself. "How can you learn lessons in here? Why, there's hardly room for *you*, and no room at all for any lesson-books!"

And so she went on, taking first one side and then the other, and making quite a conversation of it altogether; but after a few minutes she heard a voice outside, and stopped to listen.

"Mary Ann! Mary Ann!" said the voice. "Fetch me my gloves

24 *If not the first, certainly the most influential Freudian reading of this and the preceding scenes was given by William Empson in* SOME VERSIONS OF PASTORAL *(1935).*

25 *This is a double-edged line and perhaps a poignant one, given Carroll's feelings about his child-friends growing up. The letters are full of self-pitying jokes on the subject: 'Some children have a most disagreeable way of getting grown-up. I hope you won't do anything of that sort before we meet again.'*

this moment!" Then came a little pattering of feet on the stairs. Alice knew it was the Rabbit coming to look for her, and she trembled till she shook the house, quite forgetting that she was now about a thousand times as large as the Rabbit, and had no reason to be afraid of him.

Presently the Rabbit came up to the door, and tried to open it; but, as the door opened inwards, and Alice's elbow was pressed hard against it, that attempt proved a failure. Alice heard him say to himself "Then I'll go round and get in at the window."

"*That* you wo'n't!" thought Alice, and after waiting till she fancied she heard the Rabbit just under the window, she suddenly spread out her hand, and made a snatch in the air. She did not get hold of anything, but she heard a little shriek and a fall, and a crash of broken glass, from which she concluded that it was just possible he had fallen into a cucumber-frame,[26] or something of the sort.

Next came an angry voice—the Rabbit's—"Pat! Pat! Where are you?" And then a voice she had never heard before, "Sure then I'm here! Digging for apples,[27] yer honour!"

"Digging for apples, indeed!" said the Rabbit angrily. "Here! Come and help me out of *this*!" (Sounds of more broken glass.)

"Now tell me, Pat, what's that in the window?"

"Sure, it's an arm, yer honour!" (He pronounced it "arrum.")

"An arm, you goose! Who ever saw one that size? Why, it fills the whole window!"

"Sure, it does, yer honour: but it's an arm for all that."

"Well, it's got no business there, at any rate: go and take it away!"

There was a long silence after this, and Alice could only hear whispers now and then; such as "Sure, I don't like it, yer honour, at all, at all!" "Do as I tell you, you coward!", and at last she spread out her hand again, and made another snatch in the air. This time there were *two* little shrieks, and more sounds of broken glass. "What a number of cucumber-frames there must be!" thought Alice. "I wonder what they'll do next! As for pulling me out of the window, I only wish they *could*! I'm sure *I* don't want to stay in here any longer!"

She waited for some time without hearing anything more: at last came a rumbling of little cart-wheels, and the sound of a good many voices all talking together: she made out the words: "Where's the other ladder?—Why, I hadn't to bring but one. Bill's got the other—Bill! Fetch it here, lad!—Here, put 'em up at

26 A cucumber-frame is a small, low lean-to device which works on a green-house principle to provide heat to the growing plants.

27 This is a play on the French term for potato, POMME DE TERRE, *literally, 'apple of the earth.'*

this corner—No, tie 'em together first—they don't reach half high enough yet—Oh, they'll do well enough. Don't be particular—Here, Bill! Catch hold of this rope—Will the roof bear?—Mind that loose slate—Oh, it's coming down! Heads below!" (a loud crash)—"Now, who did that?—It was Bill, I fancy—Who's to go down the chimney?—Nay, *I* sha'n't! *You* do it!—*That* I wo'n't, then!—Bill's to go down—Here, Bill! The master says you've to go down the chimney!"

"Oh! So Bill's got to come down the chimney, has he?" said Alice to herself. "Why, they seem to put everything upon Bill! I wouldn't be in Bill's place for a good deal: this fireplace is narrow, to be sure; but I *think* I can kick a little!"

She drew her foot as far down the chimney as she could, and waited till she heard a little animal (she couldn't guess of what sort it was) scratching and scrambling about in the chimney close above her: then, saying to herself "This is Bill", she gave one sharp kick, and waited to see what would happen next.

The first thing she heard was a general chorus of "There goes Bill!" then the Rabbit's voice alone—"Catch him, you by the hedge!" then silence, and then another confusion of voices—"Hold up his head—Brandy now— Don't choke him—How was it, old fellow? What happened to you? Tell us all about it!"

Last came a little feeble, squeaking voice ("That's Bill," thought Alice), "Well, I hardly know—No more, thank ye; I'm better now—but I'm a deal too flustered to tell you—all I know is, something comes at me like a Jack-in-the-box, and up I goes like a sky-rocket!"

"So you did, old fellow!" said the others.

"We must burn the house down!" said the Rabbit's voice. And Alice called out, as loud as she could, "If you do, I'll set Dinah at you!"

There was a dead silence instantly, and Alice thought to herself "I wonder what they *will* do next! If they had any sense, they'd take the roof off." After a minute or two, they began moving about again, and Alice heard the Rabbit say "A barrowful will do, to begin with."

"A barrowful of *what*?" thought Alice. But she had not long to doubt, for the next moment a shower of little pebbles came rattling in at the window, and some of them hit her in the face. "I'll put a stop to this," she said to herself, and shouted out "You'd better not do that again!", which produced another dead silence.

Alice noticed, with some surprise, that the pebbles were all turning into little cakes as they lay on the floor, and a bright idea came into her head. "If I eat one of these cakes," she thought, "it's sure to make *some* change in my size; and, as it ca'n't possibly make me larger, it must make me smaller, I suppose."

So she swallowed one of the cakes,

* * * * * * * * * * *

and was delighted to find that she began shrinking directly. As soon as she was small enough to get through the door, she ran out of the house, and found quite a crowd of little animals and birds waiting outside. The poor little Lizard, Bill, was in the middle, being held up by two guinea-pigs, who were giving him something out of a bottle. They all made a rush at Alice the moment she appeared; but she ran off as hard as she could, and soon found herself safe in a thick wood.

"The first thing I've got to do," said Alice to herself, as she wandered about in the wood, "is to grow to my right size again; and the second thing is to find my way into that lovely garden. I think that will be the best plan."

It sounded an excellent plan, no doubt, and very neatly and simply arranged: the only difficulty was, that she had not the smallest idea how to set about it; and, while she was peering about anxiously among the trees, a little sharp bark just over her head made her look up in a great hurry.

An enormous puppy was looking down at her with large round eyes, and feebly stretching out one paw, trying to touch her. "Poor little thing!" said Alice, in a coaxing tone, and she tried hard to whistle to it; but she was terribly frightened all the time at the thought that it might be hungry, in which case it would be very likely to eat her up in spite of all her coaxing.

Hardly knowing what she did, she picked up a little bit of stick, and held it out to the puppy: whereupon the puppy jumped into the air off all its feet at once, with a yelp of delight, and rushed at the stick, and made believe to worry it: then Alice dodged behind a great thistle, to keep herself from being run over: and, the moment she appeared on the other side, the puppy made another rush at the stick, and tumbled head over heels in its hurry to get hold of it: then Alice, thinking it was very like having a game of play with a cart-horse, and expecting every moment to be trampled under its feet, ran round the thistle again: then the puppy began

a series of short charges at the stick, running a very little way forwards each time and a long way back, and barking hoarsely all the while, till at last it sat down a good way off, panting, with its tongue hanging out of its mouth, and its great eyes half shut.

This seemed to Alice a good opportunity for making her escape: so she set off at once, and ran till she was quite tired and out of breath, and till the puppy's bark sounded quite faint in the distance.

"And yet what a dear little puppy it was!" said Alice, as she leant against a buttercup to rest herself, and fanned herself with one of the leaves. "I should have liked teaching it tricks very much, if—if I'd only been the right size to do it! Oh dear! I'd nearly forgotten that I've got to grow up again! Let me see—how *is* it to be managed? I suppose I ought to eat or drink something or other; but the great question is 'What?' "

The great question certainly was "What?" Alice looked all round her at the flowers and the blades of grass, but she could not see anything that looked like the right thing to eat or drink under the circumstances. There was a large mushroom growing near her, about the same height as herself; and, when she had looked under it, and on both sides of it, and behind it, it occurred to her that she might as well look and see what was on top of it.

She stretched herself up on tiptoe, and peeped over the edge of the mushroom, and her eyes immediately met those of a large blue caterpillar, that was sitting on the top, with its arms folded, quietly smoking a long hookah, and taking not the smallest notice of her or of anything else.

V

Advice from a Caterpillar

The Caterpillar and Alice looked at each other for some time in silence: at last the Caterpillar took the hookah out of its mouth, and addressed her in a languid, sleepy voice.

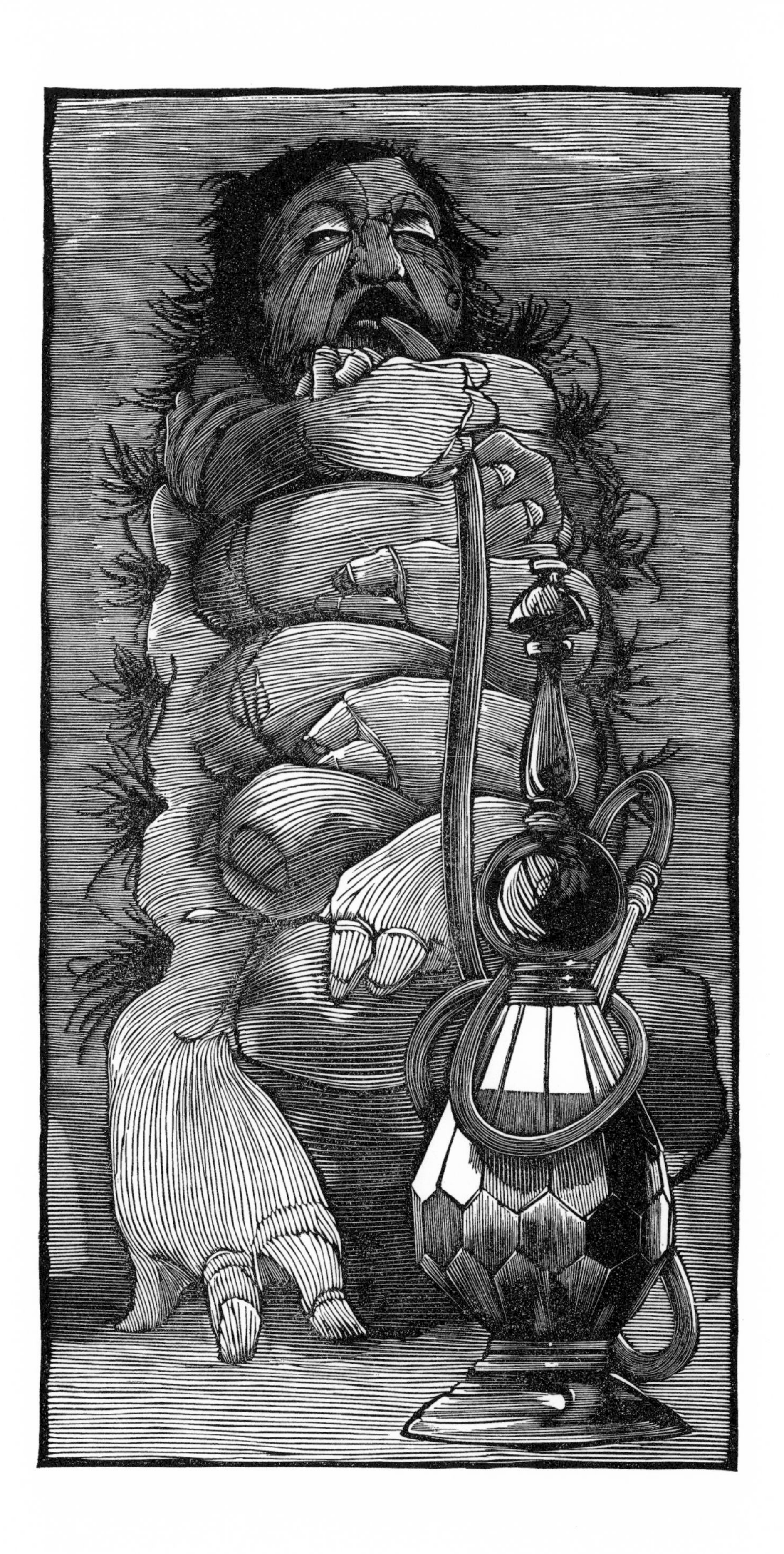

"Who are *you*?" said the Caterpillar.

This was not an encouraging opening for a conversation. Alice replied, rather shyly, "I—I hardly know, Sir, just at present—at least I know who I *was* when I got up this morning, but I think I must have been changed several times since then."

"What do you mean by that?" said the Caterpillar, sternly. "Explain yourself!"

"I ca'n't explain *myself*, I'm afraid, Sir," said Alice, "because I'm not myself, you see."

"I don't see," said the Caterpillar.

"I'm afraid I ca'n't put it more clearly," Alice replied, very politely, "for I ca'n't understand it myself, to begin with; and being so many different sizes in a day is very confusing."

"It isn't," said the Caterpillar.

"Well, perhaps you haven't found it so yet," said Alice; "but when you have to turn into a chrysalis—you will some day, you know—and then after that into a butterfly, I should think you'll feel it a little queer, wo'n't you?"

"Not a bit," said the Caterpillar.

"Well, perhaps *your* feelings may be different," said Alice: "all I know is, it would feel very queer to *me*."

"You!" said the Caterpillar contemptuously. "Who are *you*?"

Which brought them back again to the beginning of the conversation. Alice felt a little irritated at the Caterpillar's making such *very* short remarks, and she drew herself up and said, very gravely, "I think you ought to tell me who *you* are, first."

"Why?" said the Caterpillar.

Here was another puzzling question; and, as Alice could not think of any good reason, and the Caterpillar seemed to be in a *very* unpleasant state of mind, she turned away.

"Come back!" the Caterpillar called after her. "I've something important to say!"

This sounded promising, certainly. Alice turned and came back again.

"Keep your temper," said the Caterpillar.

"Is that all?" said Alice, swallowing down her anger as well as she could.

"No," said the Caterpillar.

Alice thought she might as well wait, as she had nothing else to do, and perhaps after all it might tell her something worth hearing. For some minutes it puffed away without speaking; but at last it unfolded its arms, took the hookah out of its mouth again, and said "So you think you're changed, do you?"

"I'm afraid I am, Sir," said Alice. "I ca'n't remember things as I used—and I don't keep the same size for ten minutes together!"

"Ca'n't remember *what* things?" said the Caterpillar.

"Well, I've tried to say *'How doth the little busy bee,'* but it all came different!" Alice replied in a very melancholy voice.

"Repeat *'You are old, Father William,'* "[28] said the Caterpillar.

Alice folded her hands, and began:—

"You are old, Father William," the young man said,
"And your hair has become very white;
And yet you incessantly stand on your head—
Do you think, at your age, it is right?"

"In my youth," Father William replied to his son,
"I feared it might injure the brain;
But, now that I'm perfectly sure I have none,
Why, I do it again and again."

"You are old," said the youth, "as I mentioned before,
And have grown most uncommonly fat;
Yet you turned a back-somersault in at the door—
Pray, what is the reason of that?"

"In my youth," said the sage, as he shook his grey locks,
"I kept all my limbs very supple
By the use of this ointment—one shilling the box—
Allow me to sell you a couple?"

"You are old," said the youth, "and your jaws are too weak
For anything tougher than suet;
Yet you finished the goose, with the bones and the beak—
Pray, how did you manage to do it?"

"In my youth," said his father, "I took to the law,
And argued each case with my wife;
And the muscular strength, which it gave to my jaw
Has lasted the rest of my life."

28 This poem parodies Robert Southey's self-parodying 'The Old Man's Comforts, and How He Gained Them' (1799), a blatantly didactic poem advising children to forgo childhood altogether and to measure thoughts and deeds against finales (not a bad summary of Alice's position). The last half of the poem is enough to provide an idea of the whole:

You are old, Father William, the young man cried,
And pleasures with youth pass away;
And yet you lament not the days that are gone,
Now tell me the reason, I pray.

In the days of my youth, Father William replied,
I remember'd that youth could not last;
I thought of the future, whatever I did,
That I never might grieve for the past.

You are old, Father William, the young man cried,
And life must be hastening away;
You are cheerful, and love to converse upon death,
Now tell me the reason, I pray.

I am cheerful, young man, Father William replied,
Let the cause thy attention engage;
In the days of my youth I remember'd my God!
And He hath not forgotten my age.

"You are old," said the youth, "one would hardly suppose
That your eye was as steady as ever;
Yet you balanced an eel on the end of your nose—
What made you so awfully clever?"

"I have answered three questions, and that is enough,"
Said his father. "Don't give yourself airs!
Do you think I can listen all day to such stuff?
Be off, or I'll kick you down-stairs!"

"That is not said right," said the Caterpillar.

"Not *quite* right, I'm afraid," said Alice, timidly: "some of the words have got altered."

"It is wrong from beginning to end," said the Caterpillar, decidedly; and there was silence for some minutes.

The Caterpillar was the first to speak.

"What size do you want to be?" it asked.

"Oh, I'm not particular as to size," Alice hastily replied; "only one doesn't like changing so often, you know."

"I *don't* know," said the Caterpillar.

Alice said nothing: she had never been so much contradicted in all her life before, and she felt that she was losing her temper.

"Are you content now?" said the Caterpillar.

"Well, I should like to be a *little* larger, Sir, if you wouldn't mind," said Alice: "three inches is such a wretched height to be."

"It is a very good height indeed!" said the Caterpillar angrily, rearing itself upright as it spoke (it was exactly three inches high).

"But I'm not used to it!" pleaded poor Alice in a piteous tone. And she thought to herself "I wish the creatures wouldn't be so easily offended!"

"You'll get used to it in time," said the Caterpillar; and it put the hookah into its mouth, and began smoking again.

This time Alice waited patiently until it chose to speak again. In a minute or two the Caterpillar took the hookah out of its mouth, and yawned once or twice, and shook itself. Then it got down off the mushroom, and crawled away into the grass, merely remarking, as it went, "One side will make you grow taller, and the other side will make you grow shorter."

"One side of *what*? The other side of *what*?" thought Alice to herself.

"Of the mushroom," said the Caterpillar, just as if she had asked it aloud; and in another moment it was out of sight.

Alice remained looking thoughtfully at the mushroom for a minute, trying to make out which were the two sides of it; and, as it was perfectly round, she found this a very difficult question.

However, at last she stretched her arms round it as far as they would go, and broke off a bit of the edge with each hand.

"And now which is which?" she said to herself, and nibbled a little of the right-hand bit to try the effect.

* * * * * * * * * * *

The next moment she felt a violent blow underneath her chin: it had struck her foot!

She was a good deal frightened by this very sudden change, but she felt that there was no time to be lost, as she was shrinking rapidly: so she set to work at once to eat some of the other bit. Her chin was pressed so closely against her foot, that there was hardly room to open her mouth; but she did it at last, and managed to swallow a morsel of the left-hand bit.

* * * * * * * * * * *

"Come, my head's free at last!" said Alice in a tone of delight, which changed into alarm in another moment, when she found that her shoulders were nowhere to be found: all she could see, when she looked down, was an immense length of neck, which seemed to rise like a stalk out of a sea of green leaves that lay far below her.

"What *can* all that green stuff be?" said Alice. "And where *have* my shoulders got to? And oh, my poor hands, how is it I ca'n't see you?" She was moving them about, as she spoke, but no result seemed to follow, except a little shaking among the distant green leaves.

As there seemed to be no chance of getting her hands up to her head, she tried to get her head down to *them*, and was delighted to find that her neck would bend about easily in any direction, like a serpent.[29] She had just succeeded in curving it down into a graceful zigzag, and was going to dive in among the leaves, which she found to be nothing but the tops of the trees under which she had been wandering, when a sharp hiss made her draw back in a

29 The simile is directly subversive in giving reinforcement-in-advance to the Pigeon's charge.

hurry: a large pigeon had flown into her face, and was beating her violently with its wings.

"Serpent!" screamed the Pigeon.

"I'm *not* a serpent!" said Alice indignantly. "Let me alone!"

"Serpent, I say again!" repeated the Pigeon, but in a more subdued tone, and added, with a kind of sob, "I've tried every way, but nothing seems to suit them!"

"I haven't the least idea what you're talking about," said Alice.

"I've tried the roots of trees, and I've tried banks, and I've tried hedges," the Pigeon went on, without attending to her; "but those serpents! There's no pleasing them!"

Alice was more and more puzzled, but she thought there was no use in saying anything more till the Pigeon had finished.

"As if it wasn't trouble enough hatching the eggs," said the Pigeon; "but I must be on the look-out for serpents, night and day! Why, I haven't had a wink of sleep these three weeks!"

"I'm very sorry you've been annoyed," said Alice, who was beginning to see its meaning.

"And just as I'd taken the highest tree in the wood," continued the Pigeon, raising its voice to a shriek, "and just as I was thinking I should be free of them at last, they must needs come wriggling down from the sky! Ugh, Serpent!"

"But I'm *not* a serpent, I tell you!" said Alice. "I'm a—I'm a——"

"Well! *What* are you?" said the Pigeon. "I can see you're trying to invent something!"

"I—I'm a little girl," said Alice, rather doubtfully, as she remembered the number of changes she had gone through, that day.

"A likely story indeed!" said the Pigeon, in a tone of the deepest contempt. "I've seen a good many little girls in my time, but never *one* with such a neck as that! No, no! You're a serpent; and there's no use denying it. I suppose you'll be telling me next that you never tasted an egg!"

"I *have* tasted eggs, certainly," said Alice, who was a very truthful child; "but little girls eat eggs quite as much as serpents do, you know."

"I don't believe it," said the Pigeon; "but if they do, why, then they're a kind of serpent: that's all I can say."

This was such a new idea to Alice, that she was quite silent for a minute or two,[30] which gave the Pigeon the opportunity of adding "You're looking for eggs, I know *that* well enough; and what does it matter to me whether you're a little girl or a serpent?"

30 *Alice, as often happens, has fallen into a logical trap and is defeated by her own weapons. Here she seeks to make a distinction between little girls and serpents—and fails.*

"It matters a good deal to *me*," said Alice hastily; "but I'm not looking for eggs, as it happens; and, if I was, I shouldn't want *yours*: I don't like them raw."

"Well, be off, then!" said the Pigeon in a sulky tone, as it settled down again into its nest. Alice crouched down among the trees as well as she could, for her neck kept getting entangled among the branches, and every now and then she had to stop and untwist it. After a while she remembered that she still held the pieces of mushroom in her hands, and she set to work very carefully, nibbling first at one and then at the other, and growing sometimes taller, and sometimes shorter, until she had succeeded in bringing herself down to her usual height.

* * * * * * * * * * *

It was so long since she had been anything near the right size, that it felt quite strange at first; but she got used to it in a few minutes, and began talking to herself, as usual, "Come, there's half my plan done now! How puzzling all these changes are! I'm never sure what I'm going to be, from one minute to another! However, I've got back to my right size: the next thing is, to get into that beautiful garden—how *is* that to be done, I wonder?" As she said this, she came suddenly upon an open place, with a little house in

it about four feet high. "Whoever lives there," thought Alice, "it'll never do to come upon them *this* size: why, I should frighten them out of their wits!" So she began nibbling at the right-hand bit again, and did not venture to go near the house till she had brought herself down to nine inches high.

* * * * * * * * * * *

VI

Pig and Pepper

For a minute or two she stood looking at the house, and wondering what to do next, when suddenly a footman in livery came running out of the wood—(she considered him to be a footman because he was in livery: otherwise, judging by his face only, she would have called him a fish)[31]—and rapped loudly at the door with his knuckles. It was opened by another footman in livery, with a round face, and large eyes like a frog; and both footmen, Alice noticed, had powdered hair that curled all over their heads. She felt very curious to know what it was all about, and crept a little way out of the wood to listen.

The Fish-Footman began by producing from under his arm a great letter, nearly as large as himself, and this he handed over to the other, saying, in a solemn tone, "For the Duchess. An invitation from the Queen to play croquet." The Frog-Footman repeated, in the same solemn tone, only changing the order of the words a little, "From the Queen. An invitation for the Duchess to play croquet."

31 *It has been suggested (by Roger Lancelyn Green) that the Fish-Footman was modeled on Bultitude, Dean Liddell's coachman.*

Then they both bowed, and their curls got entangled together.

Alice laughed so much at this, that she had to run back into the wood for fear of their hearing her; and, when she next peeped out, the Fish-Footman was gone, and the other was sitting on the ground near the door, staring stupidly up into the sky.

Alice went timidly up to the door, and knocked.

"There's no sort of use in knocking," said the Footman, "and that for two reasons. First, because I'm on the same side of the door as you are: secondly, because they're making such a noise inside, no one could possibly hear you." And certainly there *was* a most extraordinary noise going on within—a constant howling and sneezing, and every now and then a great crash, as if a dish or kettle had been broken to pieces.

"Please, then," said Alice, "how am I to get in?"

"There might be some sense in your knocking," the Footman went on, without attending to her, "if we had the door between us. For instance, if you were *inside*, you might knock, and I could let you out, you know." He was looking up into the sky all the time he was speaking, and this Alice thought decidedly uncivil. "But perhaps he ca'n't help it," she said to herself; "his eyes are so *very* nearly at the top of his head. But at any rate he might answer questions.—How am I to get in?" she repeated, aloud.

"I shall sit here," the Footman remarked, "till to-morrow——"

At this moment the door of the house opened, and a large plate came skimming out, straight at the Footman's head: it just grazed his nose, and broke to pieces against one of the trees behind him.

"——or next day, maybe," the Footman continued in the same tone, exactly as if nothing had happened.

"How am I to get in?" asked Alice again, in a louder tone.

"*Are* you to get in at all?" said the Footman. "That's the first question, you know."

It was, no doubt: only Alice did not like to be told so. "It's really dreadful," she muttered to herself, "the way all the creatures argue. It's enough to drive one crazy!"

The Footman seemed to think this a good opportunity for repeating his remark, with variations. "I shall sit here," he said, "on and off, for days and days."

"But what am *I* to do?" said Alice.

"Anything you like," said the Footman, and began whistling.

"Oh, there's no use in talking to him," said Alice desperately: "he's perfectly idiotic!" And she opened the door and went in.

The door led right into a large kitchen, which was full of smoke from one end to the other: the Duchess was sitting on a three-legged stool in the middle, nursing a baby: the cook was leaning over the fire, stirring a large cauldron which seemed to be full of soup.

"There's certainly too much pepper in that soup!" Alice said to herself, as well as she could for sneezing.

There was certainly too much of it in the *air*. Even the Duchess sneezed occasionally; and the baby was sneezing and howling alternately without a moment's pause. The only things in the kitchen, that did *not* sneeze, were the cook, and a large cat, which was lying on the hearth and grinning from ear to ear.

"Please would you tell me," said Alice, a little timidly, for she was not quite sure whether it was good manners for her to speak first, "why your cat grins like that?"

"It's a Cheshire-Cat,"[32] said the Duchess, "and that's why. Pig!"

She said the last word with such sudden violence that Alice quite jumped; but she saw in another moment that it was addressed to the baby, and not to her, so she took courage, and went on again:—

"I didn't know that Cheshire-Cats always grinned; in fact, I didn't know that cats *could* grin."

"They all can," said the Duchess; "and most of 'em do."

"I don't know of any that do," Alice said very politely, feeling quite pleased to have got into a conversation.

"You don't know much," said the Duchess; "and that's a fact."

Alice did not at all like the tone of this remark, and thought it would be as well to introduce some other subject of conversation. While she was trying to fix on one, the cook took the cauldron of soup off the fire, and at once set to work throwing everything within her reach at the Duchess and the baby—the fire-irons came first; then followed a shower of saucepans, plates, and dishes. The Duchess took no notice of them even when they hit her; and the baby was howling so much already, that it was quite impossible to say whether the blows hurt it or not.

"Oh, *please* mind what you're doing!" cried Alice, jumping up and down in an agony of terror. "Oh, there goes his *precious* nose!", as an unusually large saucepan flew close by it, and very nearly carried it off.

"If everybody minded their own business," the Duchess said, in a hoarse growl, "the world would go round a deal faster than it does."

"Which would *not* be an advantage," said Alice, who felt very glad to get an opportunity of showing off a little of her knowledge. "Just think what work it would make with the day and night! You see the earth takes twenty-four hours to turn round on its axis——"[33]

"Talking of axes," said the Duchess, "chop off her head!"

Alice glanced rather anxiously at the cook, to see if she meant to take the hint; but the cook was busily engaged in stirring the soup, and did not seem to be listening, so she ventured to go on again: "Twenty-four hours, I *think*; or is it twelve? I——"

32 There is some controversy about the origins of the phrase, 'grin like a Cheshire cat.' Carroll may have seen a scholarly note arguing that the saying referred to Cheshire cheeses made in the form of grinning cats, an ingenious idea since declared groundless. Another possibility is that one of the leading families of Cheshire had as part of their coat of arms the face of a lion and that gradually, through the work of local and unskilled sign painters, the lion began to look like a grinning cat. Dubious, but less improbable than many whoppers told in the unlicensed sport of hunting the roots of proverbs.

33 Alice here is taking on the manner of the governesses and is thus set up for the Duchess' punning rebuke.

"Oh, don't bother *me!*" said the Duchess. "I never could abide figures!" And with that she began nursing her child again, singing a sort of lullaby to it as she did so, and giving it a violent shake at the end of every line:—

"Speak roughly to your little boy,
And beat him when he sneezes:
He only does it to annoy,
Because he knows it teases."

CHORUS.
(in which the cook and the baby joined):—
"Wow! Wow! Wow!"

While the Duchess sang the second verse of the song, she kept tossing the baby violently up and down, and the poor little thing howled so, that Alice could hardly hear the words:—

"I speak severely to my boy,
I beat him when he sneezes;
For he can thoroughly enjoy
The pepper when he pleases!"[34]

CHORUS.
"Wow! Wow! Wow!"[35]

"Here! You may nurse it a bit, if you like!" the Duchess said to Alice, flinging the baby at her as she spoke. "I must go and get ready to play croquet with the Queen," and she hurried out of the room. The cook threw a frying-pan after her as she went out, but it just missed her.

Alice caught the baby with some difficulty, as it was a queer-shaped little creature, and held out its arms and legs in all directions, "just like a star-fish," thought Alice. The poor little thing was snorting like a steam-engine when she caught it, and kept doubling itself up and straightening itself out again, so that altogether, for the first minute or two, it was as much as she could do to hold it.

As soon as she had made out the proper way of nursing it (which was to twist it up into a sort of knot, and then keep tight hold of its right ear and left foot, so as to prevent its undoing

34 *As Carroll said in a letter, 'One of the deepest motives (as you are aware) in the human breast . . . is Alliteration.'*

35 *The poem parodies a popular children's poem published in 1848, probably written by David Bates, though originally attributed to G.W. Langford. The original agrees with Sairey Gamp that life is a 'wale of tears,' though it departs from her feelings in suggesting that one should respond to this misery by treating children with a quavering, incubator-like gentleness:*

Speak gently to the little child!
Its love be sure to gain;
Teach it in accents soft and mild—
It may not long remain.

itself), she carried it out into the open air. "If I don't take this child away with me," thought Alice, "they're sure to kill it in a day or two. Wouldn't it be murder to leave it behind?" She said the last words out loud, and the little thing grunted in reply (it had left off sneezing by this time). "Don't grunt," said Alice; "that's not at all a proper way of expressing yourself."

The baby grunted again, and Alice looked very anxiously into its face to see what was the matter with it. There could be no doubt that it had a *very* turn-up nose, much more like a snout than a real nose: also its eyes were getting extremely small for a baby: altogether Alice did not like the look of the thing at all. "But perhaps it was only sobbing," she thought, and looked into its eyes again, to see if there were any tears.

No, there were no tears. "If you're going to turn into a pig, my dear," said Alice, seriously, "I'll have nothing more to do with you. Mind now!" The poor little thing sobbed again (or grunted, it was impossible to say which), and they went on for some while in silence.

Alice was just beginning to think to herself "Now, what am I to do with this creature, when I get it home?" when it grunted again, so violently, that she looked down into its face in some alarm. This time there could be *no* mistake about it: it was neither more nor less than a pig, and she felt that it would be quite absurd for her to carry it any further.

So she set the little creature down, and felt quite relieved to see it trot away quietly into the wood. "If it had grown up," she said to herself, "it would have made a dreadfully ugly child: but it makes rather a handsome pig, I think." And she began thinking over other children she knew, who might do very well as pigs, and was just saying to herself "if one only knew the right way to change them——" when she was a little startled by seeing the Cheshire-Cat sitting on a bough of a tree a few yards off.

The Cat only grinned when it saw Alice. It looked good-natured, she thought: still it had *very* long claws and a great many teeth, so she felt that it ought to be treated with respect.

"Cheshire-Puss," she began, rather timidly, as she did not at all know whether it would like the name: however, it only grinned a little wider. "Come, it's pleased so far," thought Alice, and she went on. "Would you tell me, please, which way I ought to go from here?"

"That depends a good deal on where you want to get to," said the Cat.

"I don't much care where——" said Alice.

"Then it doesn't matter which way you go," said the Cat.

"——so long as I get *somewhere*," Alice added as an explanation.

"Oh, you're sure to do that," said the Cat, "if you only walk long enough."

Alice felt that this could not be denied, so she tried another question. "What sort of people live about here?"

"In *that* direction," the Cat said, waving its right paw round, "lives a Hatter: and in *that* direction," waving the other paw, "lives a March Hare. Visit either you like: they're both mad."[36]

"But I don't want to go among mad people," Alice remarked.

"Oh, you ca'n't help that," said the Cat: "we're all mad here. I'm mad. You're mad."[37]

"How do you know I'm mad?" said Alice.

"You must be," said the Cat, "or you wouldn't have come here."

Alice didn't think that proved it at all: however, she went on. "And how do you know that you're mad?"

"To begin with," said the Cat, "a dog's not mad. You grant that?"

"I suppose so," said Alice.

"Well, then," the Cat went on, "you see a dog growls when it's

36 'Mad as a hatter' is a proverbial expression, apparently first used in the nineteenth century. Explanations of its origins commonly refer to the fact that the mercury used in making felt caused hat-makers' muscles to jerk spasmodically, simulating popular notions of Bedlamite behavior. Probably less convincing is the argument that the phrase is a corruption of the French IL RAISSONE COMME UNE HUITRE *('He reasons like an oyster'). It is interesting, if perhaps irrelevant, that 'hatter' and 'March hare' join company in the* OED *with a list of 'mad as a——' phrases suitable in its bizarre way for Wonderland: bucke, weaver, cut snake, Ajax, meat axe, and wet hen.*

It has been suggested that the Mad Hatter was modeled on Theophilus Carter, an Oxford furniture dealer once connected with Christ Church. There is a story (unproven) that Tenniel was taken by Carroll to see Carter in preparation for drawing the Hatter. Carter, who stood in front of his store wearing a very large hat, was a man of ideas, inventing, among other things, an Alarm Clock Bed, which tipped its owner out onto the floor on cue. Though it achieved the distinction of being exhibited at the Crystal Palace in 1851, the bed failed to gain the popularity which was its due, partly, perhaps, because it seems often to have misfired in the middle of the night.

'Mad as a March hare,' an old proverbial saying, probably derives from the fact, if that's what it is, that, in the mating season (March), hares, like other British life forms, are unusually wild. Erasmus, however, used the phrase 'mad as a marsh hare,' explaining that 'hares are wilder in marshes from the absence of hedges and cover.' Perhaps the present version is a corruption of the 'marsh' form, though there is undoubted appeal in the mating argument. Alice's later comment on the Hare being a little less mad since it is May seems to settle the matter as far as this text is concerned.

37 Carroll refers in a letter to a complementary Irish saying about two muddy roads: 'Whichever you choose, you'll soon be wishing you had taken the other!'

angry, and wags its tail when it's pleased. Now *I* growl when I'm pleased, and wag my tail when I'm angry. Therefore I'm mad."

"*I* call it purring, not growling," said Alice.

"Call it what you like," said the Cat. "Do you play croquet with the Queen to-day?"

"I should like it very much," said Alice, "but I haven't been invited yet."

"You'll see me there," said the Cat, and vanished.

Alice was not much surprised at this, she was getting so used to queer things happening. While she was still looking at the place where it had been, it suddenly appeared again.

"By-the-bye, what became of the baby?" said the Cat. "I'd nearly forgotten to ask."

"It turned into a pig," Alice quietly said, just as if it had come back in a natural way.

"I thought it would," said the Cat, and vanished again.

Alice waited a little, half expecting to see it again, but it did not appear, and after a minute or two she walked on in the direction in which the March Hare was said to live. "I've seen hatters before," she said to herself: "the March Hare will be much the most interesting, and perhaps, as this is May, it won't be raving mad—at least not so mad as it was in March." As she said this, she looked up, and there was the Cat again, sitting on a branch of a tree.

"Did you say 'pig', or 'fig'?" said the Cat.

"I said 'pig'," replied Alice; "and I wish you wouldn't keep appearing and vanishing so suddenly: you make one quite giddy!"

"All right," said the Cat; and this time it vanished quite slowly, beginning with the end of the tail, and ending with the grin, which remained some time after the rest of it had gone.

"Well! I've often seen a cat without a grin," thought Alice; "but a grin without a cat! It's the most curious thing I ever saw in all my life!"

She had not gone much farther before she came in sight of the house of the March Hare: she thought it must be the right house, because the chimneys were shaped like ears and the roof was thatched with fur. It was so large a house, that she did not like to go nearer till she had nibbled some more of the left-hand bit of mushroom,

*   *   *   *   *   *   *   *   *   *   *

and raised herself to about two feet high: even then she walked up towards it rather timidly, saying to herself "Suppose it should be raving mad after all! I almost wish I'd gone to see the Hatter instead!"

VII

A Mad Tea-Party

There was a table set out under a tree in front of the house, and the March Hare and the Hatter were having tea at it: a Dormouse[38] was sitting between them, fast asleep, and the other two were resting their elbows on it, and talking over its head. "Very uncomfortable for the Dormouse," thought Alice; "only as it's asleep, I suppose it doesn't mind."

The table was a large one, but the three were all crowded together at one corner of it. "No room! No room!" they cried out when they saw Alice coming. "There's *plenty* of room!" said Alice indignantly, and she sat down in a large arm-chair at one end of the table.

"Have some wine," the March Hare said in an encouraging tone.

Alice looked all round the table, but there was nothing on it but tea. "I don't see any wine," she remarked.

"There isn't any," said the March Hare.

"Then it wasn't very civil of you to offer it," said Alice angrily.

"It wasn't very civil of you to sit down without being invited," said the March Hare.

"I didn't know it was *your* table," said Alice: "it's laid for a great many more than three."

"Your hair wants cutting," said the Hatter. He had been looking at Alice for some time with great curiosity, and this was his first speech.

"You should learn not to make personal remarks," Alice said with some severity: "it's very rude."

The Hatter opened his eyes very wide on hearing this; but all he *said* was "Why is a raven like a writing-desk?"[39]

"Come, we shall have some fun now!" thought Alice. "I'm glad

38 *A dormouse is a small rodent that hibernates in the winter and is also nocturnal, thus a convenient image, used for centuries in England, for a sluggard or a person given to daytime dozing.*

39 *In the Preface to the 1897 edition Carroll gave an answer to the riddle: 'Because it can produce a few notes, though they are* VERY *flat; and it is nevar put with the wrong end in front!' He added, however, that 'the Riddle, as originally invented, had no answer at all.' Many other solutions have been suggested.*

they've begun asking riddles—I believe I can guess that," she added aloud.

"Do you mean that you think you can find out the answer to it?" said the March Hare.

"Exactly so," said Alice.

"Then you should say what you mean," the March Hare went on.

"I do," Alice hastily replied; "at least—at least I mean what I say—that's the same thing, you know."

"Not the same thing a bit!" said the Hatter. "You might just as well say that 'I see what I eat' is the same thing as 'I eat what I see'!"

"You might just as well say," added the March Hare, "that 'I like what I get' is the same thing as 'I get what I like'!"

"You might just as well say," added the Dormouse, which seemed to be talking in its sleep, "that 'I breathe when I sleep' is the same thing as 'I sleep when I breathe'!"

"It *is* the same thing with you," said the Hatter, and here the conversation dropped, and the party sat silent for a minute, while Alice thought over all she could remember about ravens and writing-desks, which wasn't much.

40 *The Cheshire Cat had previously remarked that the month is May; this new information establishes the date as May fourth, Alice Liddell's birthday.*

The Hatter was the first to break the silence. "What day of the month is it?" he said, turning to Alice: he had taken his watch out of his pocket, and was looking at it uneasily, shaking it every now and then, and holding it to his ear.

Alice considered a little, and then said "The fourth."[40]

"Two days wrong!" sighed the Hatter. "I told you butter wouldn't suit the works!" he added, looking angrily at the March Hare.

"It was the *best* butter," the March Hare meekly replied.

"Yes, but some crumbs must have got in as well," the Hatter grumbled: "you shouldn't have put it in with the bread-knife."

The March Hare took the watch and looked at it gloomily: then he dipped it into his cup of tea, and looked at it again: but he could think of nothing better to say than his first remark, "It was the *best* butter, you know."

Alice had been looking over his shoulder with some curiosity. "What a funny watch!" she remarked. "It tells the day of the month, and doesn't tell what o'clock it is!"

"Why should it?" muttered the Hatter. "Does *your* watch tell you what year it is?"

"Of course not," Alice replied very readily: "but that's because it stays the same year for such a long time together."

"Which is just the case with *mine*," said the Hatter.

Alice felt dreadfully puzzled. The Hatter's remark seemed to have no meaning in it, and yet it was certainly English. "I don't quite understand," she said, as politely as she could.

"The Dormouse is asleep again," said the Hatter, and he poured a little hot tea upon its nose.

The Dormouse shook its head impatiently, and said, without opening its eyes, "Of course, of course: just what I was going to remark myself."

"Have you guessed the riddle yet?" the Hatter said, turning to Alice again.

"No, I give it up," Alice replied. "What's the answer?"

"I haven't the slightest idea," said the Hatter.

"Nor I," said the March Hare.

Alice sighed wearily. "I think you might do something better with the time," she said, "than waste it asking riddles with no answers."

"If you knew Time as well as I do," said the Hatter, "you wouldn't talk about wasting *it*. It's *him*."

"I don't know what you mean," said Alice.

"Of course you don't!" the Hatter said, tossing his head contemptuously. "I dare say you never even spoke to Time!"

"Perhaps not," Alice cautiously replied; "but I know I have to beat time when I learn music."

"Ah! That accounts for it," said the Hatter. "He wo'n't stand beating. Now, if you only kept on good terms with him, he'd do almost anything you liked with the clock. For instance, suppose it were nine o'clock in the morning, just time to begin lessons: you'd only have to whisper a hint to Time, and round goes the clock in a twinkling! Half-past one, time for dinner!"

("I only wish it was," the March Hare said to himself in a whisper.)

"That would be grand, certainly," said Alice thoughtfully; "but then—I shouldn't be hungry for it, you know."

"Not at first, perhaps," said the Hatter: "but you could keep it to half-past one as long as you liked."

"Is that the way *you* manage?" Alice asked.

The Hatter shook his head mournfully. "Not I!" he replied. "We quarreled last March—just before *he* went mad, you know——" (pointing with his teaspoon at the March Hare,) "——it was at the great concert given by the Queen of Hearts, and I had to sing

'Twinkle, twinkle, little bat!
How I wonder what you're at!'

You know the song, perhaps?"

"I've heard something like it," said Alice.

"It goes on, you know," the Hatter continued, "in this way:—

'Up above the world you fly,
Like a tea-tray in the sky.
Twinkle, twinkle—' "[41]

41 *This poem is a parody of* 'The Star,' *written by Jane Taylor and published in* RHYMES FOR THE NURSERY (1806). *The first stanza still lives, as a highly popular nursery rhyme in England and to torture those beginning musical instrument instruction in America:*

Twinkle, twinkle, little star,
How I wonder what you are!
Up above the world so high,
Like a diamond in the sky.

Professor Bartholomew Price, Dodgson's tutor at Whitby in 1854 and later Master of Pembroke, was nicknamed 'Bat.'

Here the Dormouse shook itself, and began singing in its sleep "*Twinkle, twinkle, twinkle, twinkle—*" and went on so long that they had to pinch it to make it stop.

"Well, I'd hardly finished the first verse," said the Hatter, "when the Queen jumped up and bawled out 'He's murdering the time! Off with his head!' "

"How dreadfully savage!" exclaimed Alice.

"And ever since that," the Hatter went on in a mournful tone, "he won't do a thing I ask! It's always six o'clock now."

A bright idea came into Alice's head. "Is that the reason so many tea-things are put out here?" she asked.

"Yes, that's it," said the Hatter with a sigh: "it's always tea-time, and we've no time to wash the things between whiles."

"Then you keep moving round, I suppose?" said Alice.

"Exactly so," said the Hatter: "as the things get used up."

"But what happens when you come to the beginning again?"[42] Alice ventured to ask.

"Suppose we change the subject," the March Hare interrupted, yawning. "I'm getting tired of this. I vote the young lady tells us a story."

"I'm afraid I don't know one," said Alice, rather alarmed at the proposal.

"Then the Dormouse shall!" they both cried. "Wake up, Dormouse!" And they pinched it on both sides at once.

The Dormouse slowly opened its eyes. "I wasn't asleep," it said in a hoarse, feeble voice, "I heard every word you fellows were saying."

"Tell us a story!" said the March Hare.

"Yes, please do!" pleaded Alice.

"And be quick about it," added the Hatter, "or you'll be asleep again before it's done."

"Once upon a time there were three little sisters," the Dormouse began in a great hurry; "and their names were Elsie, Lacie, and Tillie;[43] and they lived at the bottom of a well——"

"What did they live on?" said Alice, who always took a great interest in questions of eating and drinking.

"They lived on treacle,"[44] said the Dormouse, after thinking a minute or two.

"They couldn't have done that, you know," Alice gently remarked. "They'd have been ill."

"So they were," said the Dormouse; "*very* ill."

42 How can the party end when it's always tea-time? Alice's search for a conclusion here is echoed later, with similar results, in a conversation with the Mock Turtle on the subject of lessons—or lessens. Dodgson seems always to have had an unusual tolerance for open-endedness: his comment on the conclusion of Tennyson's THE CUP *was that it showed 'an almost morbid fondness for roundness and finish.'*

43 This is another of the private jokes: Elsie is L. C. (Lorina Charlotte), Lacie is an anagram of Alice, and Tillie is Matilda, a family nickname for Edith. There is also a play on Liddell (rhymes with 'fiddle') sisters and 'little sisters.'

44 Treacle is a black molasses produced in the refining of sugar.

Alice tried a little to fancy to herself what such an extraordinary way of living would be like, but it puzzled her too much: so she went on: "But why did they live at the bottom of a well?"

"Take some more tea," the March Hare said to Alice, very earnestly.

"I've had nothing yet," Alice replied in an offended tone: "so I ca'n't take more."

"You mean you ca'n't take *less*," said the Hatter: "it's very easy to take *more* than nothing."

"Nobody asked *your* opinion," said Alice.

"Who's making personal remarks now?" the Hatter asked triumphantly.

Alice did not quite know what to say to this: so she helped herself to some tea and bread-and-butter, and then turned to the Dormouse, and repeated her question. "Why did they live at the bottom of a well?"

The Dormouse again took a minute or two to think about it, and then said "It was a treacle-well."

"There's no such thing!" Alice was beginning very angrily, but the Hatter and the March Hare went "Sh! Sh!" and the Dormouse sulkily remarked "If you ca'n't be civil, you'd better finish the story for yourself."

"No, please go on!" Alice said. "I wo'n't interrupt you again. I dare say there may be *one*."

"One, indeed!" said the Dormouse indignantly. However, he consented to go on. "And so these three little sisters—they were learning to draw, you know——"

"What did they draw?" said Alice, quite forgetting her promise.

"Treacle," said the Dormouse, without considering at all, this time.

"I want a clean cup," interrupted the Hatter: "let's all move one place on."

He moved on as he spoke, and the Dormouse followed him: the March Hare moved into the Dormouse's place, and Alice rather unwillingly took the place of the March Hare. The Hatter was the only one who got any advantage from the change; and Alice was a good deal worse off, as the March Hare had just upset the milk-jug into his plate.

Alice did not wish to offend the Dormouse again, so she began very cautiously: "But I don't understand. Where did they draw the treacle from?"

"You can draw water out of a water-well," said the Hatter; "so I should think you could draw treacle out of a treacle-well—eh, stupid?"

"But they were *in* the well," Alice said to the Dormouse, not choosing to notice this last remark.

"Of course they were," said the Dormouse: "well in."

This answer so confused poor Alice, that she let the Dormouse go on for some time without interrupting it.

"They were learning to draw," the Dormouse went on, yawning and rubbing its eyes, for it was getting very sleepy; "and they drew all manner of things—everything that begins with an M——"

"Why with an M?" said Alice.

"Why not?" said the March Hare.

Alice was silent.

The Dormouse had closed its eyes by this time, and was going off into a doze; but, on being pinched by the Hatter, it woke up again with a little shriek, and went on: "——that begins with an M, such as mouse-traps, and the moon, and memory, and muchness—you know you say things are 'much of a muchness'—did you ever see such a thing as a drawing of a muchness?"[45]

45 The primary meaning is 'much of the same importance or value,' with implications of uniform mediocrity. It can also suggest excess or redundancy.

"Really, now you ask me," said Alice, very much confused, "I don't think——"

"Then you shouldn't talk," said the Hatter.

This piece of rudeness was more than Alice could bear: she got up in great disgust, and walked off: the Dormouse fell asleep instantly, and neither of the others took the least notice of her going, though she looked back once or twice, half hoping that they would call after her: the last time she saw them, they were trying to put the Dormouse into the teapot.

"At any rate I'll never go *there* again!" said Alice, as she picked her way through the wood. "It's the stupidest tea-party I ever was at in all my life!"

Just as she said this, she noticed that one of the trees had a door leading right into it. "That's very curious!" she thought. "But everything's curious to-day. I think I may as well go in at once." And in she went.

Once more she found herself in the long hall, and close to the little glass table. "Now, I'll manage better this time," she said to herself, and began by taking the little golden key, and unlocking

the door that led into the garden. Then she set to work nibbling at the mushroom (she had kept a piece of it in her pocket)

* * * * * * * * * * *

till she was about a foot high; then she walked down the little passage: and *then*—she found herself at last in the beautiful garden, among the bright flower-beds and the cool fountains.

VIII

The Queen's Croquet-Ground

A large rose-tree stood near the entrance of the garden: the roses growing on it were white, but there were three gardeners at it, busily painting them red. Alice thought this a very curious thing, and she went nearer to watch them, and, just as she came up to them, she heard one of them say "Look out now, Five! Don't go splashing paint over me like that!"

"I couldn't help it," said Five, in a sulky tone. "Seven jogged my elbow."

On which Seven looked up and said "That's right, Five! Always lay the blame on others!"

"*You'd* better not talk!" said Five. "I heard the Queen say only yesterday you deserved to be beheaded."

"What for?" said the one who had first spoken.

"That's none of *your* business, Two!" said Seven.

"Yes, it *is* his business!" said Five. "And I'll tell him—it was for bringing the cook tulip-roots instead of onions."

Seven flung down his brush, and had just begun "Well, of all the unjust things—" when his eye chanced to fall upon Alice, as she stood watching them, and he checked himself suddenly: the others looked round also, and all of them bowed low.

"Would you tell me," said Alice, a little timidly, "why you are painting those roses?"

Five and Seven said nothing, but looked at Two. Two began, in a low voice, "Why, the fact is, you see, Miss, this here ought to have been a *red* rose-tree, and we put a white one in by mistake; and, if the Queen was to find out, we should all have our heads cut off, you know. So you see, Miss, we're doing our best, afore she comes, to—" At this moment, Five, who had been anxiously looking across the garden, called out "The Queen! The Queen!", and

the three gardeners instantly threw themselves flat upon their faces. There was a sound of many footsteps, and Alice looked round, eager to see the Queen.

First came ten soldiers carrying clubs: these were all shaped like the three gardeners, oblong and flat, with their hands and feet at the corners: next the ten courtiers: these were ornamented all over with diamonds, and walked two and two, as the soldiers did. After these came the royal children: there were ten of them, and the little dears came jumping merrily along, hand in hand, in couples: they were all ornamented with hearts. Next came the guests, mostly Kings and Queens, and among them Alice recognized the White Rabbit: he was talking in a hurried nervous manner, smiling at everything that was said, and went by without noticing her. Then followed the Knave of Hearts, carrying the King's crown on a crimson velvet cushion; and, last of all this grand procession, came THE KING AND QUEEN OF HEARTS.[46]

46 Carroll later called the Queen of Hearts 'a sort of embodiment of ungovernable passion – a blind and aimless Fury.'

Alice was rather doubtful whether she ought not to lie down on her face like the three gardeners, but she could not remember ever having heard of such a rule at processions; "and besides, what would be the use of a procession," thought she, "if people had all to lie down upon their faces, so that they couldn't see it?" So she stood still where she was, and waited.

When the procession came opposite to Alice, they all stopped and looked at her, and the Queen said, severely, "Who is this?" She said it to the Knave of Hearts, who only bowed and smiled in reply.

"Idiot!" said the Queen, tossing her head impatiently; and, turning to Alice, she went on: "What's your name, child?"

"My name is Alice, so please your Majesty," said Alice very politely; but she added, to herself, "Why, they're only a pack of cards, after all. I needn't be afraid of them!"[47]

47 This is the first signal that Alice will escape from or find control over her adventures only through language, a somewhat ironic strategy, given that our assumptions about language have been relentlessly undermined throughout. See Donald Rackin's 'Alice's Journey to the End of Night' (PMLA, 1966).

"And who are *these*?" said the Queen, pointing to the three gardeners who were lying round the rose-tree; for, you see, as they were lying on their faces, and the pattern on their backs was the same as the rest of the pack, she could not tell whether they were gardeners, or soldiers, or courtiers, or three of her own children.

"How should *I* know?" said Alice, surprised at her own courage. "It's no business of *mine*."

The Queen turned crimson with fury, and, after glaring at her for a moment like a wild beast, screamed "Off with her head! Off with——"

"Nonsense!" said Alice, very loudly and decidedly, and the Queen was silent.

The King laid his hand upon her arm, and timidly said "Consider, my dear: she is only a child!"

The Queen turned angrily away from him, and said to the Knave "Turn them over!"

The Knave did so, very carefully, with one foot.

"Get up!" said the Queen in a shrill, loud voice, and the three gardeners instantly jumped up, and began bowing to the King, the Queen, the royal children, and everybody else.

"Leave off that!" screamed the Queen. "You make me giddy." And then, turning to the rose-tree, she went on "What *have* you been doing here?"

"May it please your Majesty," said Two, in a very humble tone, going down on one knee as he spoke, "we were trying—"

"*I* see!" said the Queen, who had meanwhile been examining the roses. "Off with their heads!" and the procession moved on, three of the soldiers remaining behind to execute the unfortunate gardeners, who ran to Alice for protection.

"You sha'n't be beheaded!" said Alice, and she put them into a large flower-pot that stood near. The three soldiers wandered about for a minute or two, looking for them, and then quietly marched off after the others.

"Are their heads off?" shouted the Queen.

"Their heads are gone, if it please your Majesty!" the soldiers shouted in reply.

"That's right!" shouted the Queen. "Can you play croquet?"

The soldiers were silent, and looked at Alice, as the question was evidently meant for her.

"Yes!" shouted Alice.

"Come on, then!" roared the Queen, and Alice joined the procession, wondering very much what would happen next.

"It's—it's a very fine day!" said a timid voice at her side. She was walking by the White Rabbit, who was peeping anxiously into her face.

"Very," said Alice. "Where's the Duchess?"

"Hush! Hush!" said the Rabbit in a low hurried tone. He looked anxiously over his shoulder as he spoke, and then raised himself upon tiptoe, put his mouth close to her ear, and whispered "She's under sentence of execution."

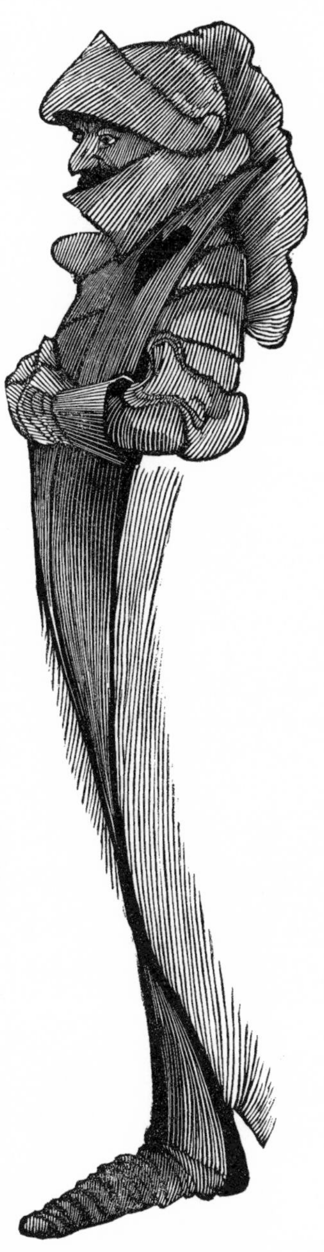

"What for?" said Alice.

"Did you say 'What a pity!'?" the Rabbit said.

"No, I didn't," said Alice. "I don't think it's at all a pity. I said 'What for?' "

"She boxed the Queen's ears—" the Rabbit began. Alice gave a little scream of laughter. "Oh, hush!" the Rabbit whispered in a frightened tone. "The Queen will hear you! You see she came rather late, and the Queen said—"

"Get to your places!" shouted the Queen in a voice of thunder, and people began running about in all directions, tumbling up against each other: however, they got settled down in a minute or two, and the game began. Alice thought she had never seen such a curious croquet-ground in all her life: it was all ridges and furrows: the croquet balls were live hedgehogs, the mallets live flamingoes,[48] and the soldiers had to double themselves up and to stand upon their hands and feet, to make the arches.

48 In ALICE'S ADVENTURES UNDER GROUND *the mallets were ostriches. Carroll, who often played croquet with the Liddell girls, later published a pamphlet,* CASTLE-CROQUET FOR FOUR PLAYERS, *giving the rules for a highly elaborate version of the game he invented. His earlier* CROQUET CASTLES (1863) *was refined as* CASTLE CROQUET *in 1866, exactly spanning the telling, writing, and publication of the story.*

The chief difficulty Alice found at first was in managing her flamingo: she succeeded in getting its body tucked away, comfortably enough, under her arm, with its legs hanging down, but generally, just as she had got its neck nicely straightened out, and was going to give the hedgehog a blow with its head, it

would twist itself round and look up in her face, with such a puzzled expression that she could not help bursting out laughing: and, when she had got its head down, and was going to begin again, it was very provoking to find that the hedgehog had unrolled itself, and was in the act of crawling away: besides all this, there was generally a ridge or a furrow in the way wherever she wanted to send the hedgehog to, and, as the doubled-up soldiers were always getting up and walking off to other parts of the ground, Alice soon came to the conclusion that it was a very difficult game indeed.

The players all played at once, without waiting for turns, quarreling all the while, and fighting for the hedgehogs; and in a very short time the Queen was in a furious passion, and went stamping about, and shouting "Off with his head!" or "Off with her head!" about once in a minute.

Alice began to feel very uneasy: to be sure, she had not as yet had any dispute with the Queen, but she knew that it might happen any minute, "and then," thought she, "what would become of me? They're dreadfully fond of beheading people here: the great wonder is that there's any one left alive!"

She was looking about for some way of escape, and wondering whether she could get away without being seen, when she noticed a curious appearance in the air: it puzzled her very much at first, but, after watching it a minute or two, she made it out to be a grin, and she said to herself "It's the Cheshire-Cat: now I shall have somebody to talk to."

"How are you getting on?" said the Cat, as soon as there was mouth enough for it to speak with.

Alice waited till the eyes appeared, and then nodded. "It's no use speaking to it," she thought, "till its ears have come, or at least one of them." In another minute the whole head appeared, and then Alice put down her flamingo, and began an account of the game, feeling very glad she had some one to listen to her. The Cat seemed to think that there was enough of it now in sight, and no more of it appeared.

"I don't think they play at all fairly," Alice began, in rather a complaining tone, "and they all quarrel so dreadfully one ca'n't hear oneself speak—and they don't seem to have any rules in particular: at least, if there are, nobody attends to them—and you've no idea how confusing it is all the things being alive: for instance, there's the arch I've got to go through next walking about at the other end of the ground—and I should have croqueted the Queen's hedgehog just now, only it ran away when it saw mine coming!"

"How do you like the Queen?" said the Cat in a low voice.

"Not at all," said Alice: "she's so extremely—" Just then she noticed that the Queen was close behind her, listening: so she went on "—likely to win, that it's hardly worth while finishing the game."

The Queen smiled and passed on.

"Who *are* you talking to?" said the King, coming up to Alice, and looking at the Cat's head with great curiosity.

"It's a friend of mine—a Cheshire-Cat," said Alice: "allow me to introduce it."

"I don't like the look of it at all," said the King: "however, it may kiss my hand, if it likes."

"I'd rather not," the Cat remarked.

"Don't be impertinent," said the King, "and don't look at me like that!" He got behind Alice as he spoke.

"A cat may look at a king,"[49] said Alice. "I've read that in some book, but I don't remember where."

"Well, it must be removed," said the King very decidedly; and he called to the Queen, who was passing at the moment, "My dear! I wish you would have this cat removed!"

The Queen had only one way of settling all difficulties, great or small. "Off with his head!" she said without even looking around.

"I'll fetch the executioner myself," said the King eagerly, and he hurried off.

Alice thought she might as well go back and see how the game was going on, as she heard the Queen's voice in the distance, screaming with passion. She had already heard her sentence three of the players to be executed for having missed their turns, and she did not like the look of things at all, as the game was in such confusion that she never knew whether it was her turn or not. So she went off in search of her hedgehog.

The hedgehog was engaged in a fight with another hedgehog, which seemed to Alice an excellent opportunity for croqueting one of them with the other: the only difficulty was, that her flamingo was gone across the other side of the garden, where Alice could see it trying in a helpless sort of way to fly up into a tree.

By the time she had caught the flamingo and brought it back, the fight was over, and both the hedgehogs were out of sight: "but it doesn't matter much," thought Alice, "as all the arches are gone from this side of the ground." So she tucked it away under her arm, that it might not escape again, and went back to have a little more conversation with her friend.

When she got back to the Cheshire-Cat, she was surprised to find quite a large crowd collected round it: there was a dispute going on between the executioner, the King, and the Queen, who were all talking at once, while all the rest were quite silent, and looked very uncomfortable.

The moment Alice appeared, she was appealed to by all three to settle the question, and they repeated their arguments to her,

49 *'A cat may look at a king' is an old proverbial saying.*

though, as they all spoke at once, she found it very hard to make out exactly what they said.

The executioner's argument was that you couldn't cut off a head unless there was a body to cut it off from: that he had never had to do such a thing before, and he wasn't going to begin at *his* time of life.

The King's argument was that anything that had a head could be beheaded, and that you weren't to talk nonsense.

The Queen's argument was that, if something wasn't done about it in less than no time, she'd have everybody executed, all round. (It was this last remark that had made the whole party look so grave and anxious.)

Alice could think of nothing else to say but "It belongs to the Duchess: you'd better ask *her* about it."

"She's in prison," the Queen said to the executioner: "fetch her here." And the executioner went off like an arrow.

The Cat's head began fading away the moment he was gone, and, by the time he had come back with the Duchess, it had entirely disappeared: so the King and the executioner ran wildly up and down, looking for it, while the rest of the party went back to the game.

IX

The Mock Turtle's Story

"You ca'n't think how glad I am to see you again, you dear old thing!" said the Duchess, as she tucked her arm affectionately into Alice's, and they walked off together.

Alice was very glad to find her in such a pleasant temper, and thought to herself that perhaps it was only the pepper that had made her so savage when they met in the kitchen.

"When *I'm* a Duchess," she said to herself (not in a very hopeful tone though), "I wo'n't have any pepper in my kitchen *at all*. Soup does very well without—Maybe it's always pepper that makes people hot-tempered," she went on, very much pleased at having found out a new kind of rule,[50] "and vinegar that makes them sour—and camomile that makes them bitter—and—and barley-sugar[51] and such things that make children sweet-tempered. I only wish people knew *that*: then they wouldn't be so stingy about it, you know——"

She had quite forgotten the Duchess by this time, and was a little startled when she heard her voice close to her ear. "You're thinking

about something, my dear, and that makes you forget to talk. I ca'n't tell you just now what the moral of that is, but I shall remember it in a bit."

"Perhaps it hasn't one," Alice ventured to remark.

"Tut, tut, child!" said the Duchess. "Everything's got a moral, if only you can find it." And she squeezed herself up closer to Alice's side as she spoke.

Alice did not much like her keeping so close to her: first, because

50 *As always, but here most explicitly, Alice is comfortable only when she can contain experience within some rule—even if the rule is absurd.*

51 *Camomile is an aromatic plant, the flowers of which were used to concoct a repulsive medicine, commonly made into a tea. Barley sugar is a candy often made in the form of twisted sticks.*

the Duchess was *very* ugly; and secondly, because she was exactly the right height to rest her chin upon Alice's shoulder, and it was an uncomfortably sharp chin. However, she did not like to be rude: so she bore it as well as she could. "The game seems to be going on rather better now," she said.

" 'Tis so," said the Duchess: "and the moral of it is—'Oh, 'tis love, 'tis love, that makes the world go round!' "

"Somebody said," whispered Alice, "that it's done by everybody minding their own business!"

"Ah well! It means much the same thing," said the Duchess, digging her sharp little chin into Alice's shoulder as she added "and the moral of *that* is—'Take care of the sense, and the sounds will take care of themselves.' "[52]

52 The traditional proverb is 'take care of the pence and the pounds will take care of themselves,' quoted, appropriately enough, by Lord Chesterfield in his LETTERS.

"How fond she is of finding morals in things!" Alice thought to herself.

"I dare say you're wondering why I don't put my arm round your waist," the Duchess said, after a pause: "the reason is, that I'm doubtful about the temper of your flamingo. Shall I try the experiment?"

"He might bite," Alice cautiously replied, not feeling at all anxious to have the experiment tried.

"Very true," said the Duchess: "flamingoes and mustard both bite. And the moral of that is—'Birds of a feather flock together.' "

"Only mustard isn't a bird," Alice remarked.

"Right, as usual," said the Duchess: "what a clear way you have of putting things!"

"It's a mineral, I *think*," said Alice.

"Of course it is," said the Duchess, who seemed ready to agree to everything that Alice said: "there's a large mustard-mine near here. And the moral of that is— 'The more there is of mine, the less there is of yours.' "[53]

53 This pointed economic proverb, apparently invented for the occasion, strikes an oblique but clearly Dickensian note quite unusual for Carroll.

"Oh, I know!" exclaimed Alice, who had not attended to this last remark. "It's a vegetable. It doesn't look like one, but it is."

"I quite agree with you," said the Duchess; "and the moral of that is—'Be what you would seem to be'—or, if you'd like it put more simply—'Never imagine yourself not to be otherwise than what it might appear to others that what you were or might have been was not otherwise than what you had been would have appeared to them to be otherwise.' "

"I think I should understand that better," Alice said very politely, "if I had it written down: but I'm afraid I ca'n't quite follow it as you say it."

"That's nothing to what I could say if I chose," the Duchess replied, in a pleased tone.

"Pray don't trouble yourself to say it any longer than that," said Alice.

"Oh, don't talk about trouble!" said the Duchess. "I make you a present of everything I've said as yet."

"A cheap sort of present!" thought Alice. "I'm glad people don't give birthday-presents like that!" But she did not venture to say it out loud.

"Thinking again?" the Duchess asked, with another dig of her sharp little chin.

"I've a right to think," said Alice sharply, for she was beginning to feel a little worried.

"Just about as much right," said the Duchess, "as pigs have to fly; and the m——"

But here, to Alice's great surprise, the Duchess' voice died away, even in the middle of her favourite word "moral," and the arm that was linked into hers began to tremble. Alice looked up, and there stood the Queen in front of them, with her arms folded, frowning like a thunderstorm.

"A fine day, your Majesty!" the Duchess began in a low, weak voice.

"Now, I give you fair warning," shouted the Queen, stamping on the ground as she spoke; "either you or your head must be off, and that in about half no time! Take your choice!"

The Duchess took her choice, and was gone in a moment.

"Let's go on with the game," the Queen said to Alice; and Alice was too much frightened to say a word, but slowly followed her back to the croquet-ground.

The other guests had taken advantage of the Queen's absence, and were resting in the shade: however, the moment they saw her, they hurried back to the game, the Queen merely remarking that a moment's delay would cost them their lives.

All the time they were playing the Queen never left off quarreling with the other players, and shouting "Off with his head!" or "Off with her head!" Those whom she sentenced were taken into custody by the soldiers, who of course had to leave off being arches to do this, so that, by the end of half an hour or so, there were no arches left, and all the players, except the King, the Queen, and Alice, were in custody and under sentence of execution.

Then the Queen left off, quite out of breath, and said to Alice "Have you seen the Mock Turtle yet?"

"No," said Alice. "I don't even know what a Mock Turtle is."

"It's the thing Mock Turtle Soup[54] is made from," said the Queen.

"I never saw one, or heard of one," said Alice.

"Come on, then," said the Queen, "and he shall tell you his history."

As they walked off together, Alice heard the King say in a low voice, to the company, generally, "You are all pardoned." "Come, *that's* a good thing!" she said to herself, for she had felt quite unhappy at the number of executions the Queen had ordered.

They very soon came upon a Gryphon,[55] lying fast asleep in the

sun. (If you don't know what a Gryphon is, look at the picture.) "Up, lazy thing!" said the Queen, "and take this young lady to see the Mock Turtle, and to hear his history. I must go back and see after some executions I have ordered," and she walked off, leaving Alice alone with the Gryphon. Alice did not quite like the look of the creature, but on the whole she thought it would be quite as safe to stay with it as to go after that savage Queen: so she waited.

54 Mock turtle itself was a dish made of a calf's head (less frequently a pig's head) dressed in such a way as to resemble a turtle. Mock turtle soup, a green soup imitating turtle soup, is also usually made of a calf's head but happily drops the difficult and grotesque camouflage.

55 A gryphon (spelled variously) is a fabulous animal with the wings of an eagle and the body of a lion who guarded the gold of Scythia.

The Gryphon sat up and rubbed its eyes: then it watched the Queen till she was out of sight: then it chuckled. "What fun!" said the Gryphon, half to itself, half to Alice.

"What *is* the fun?" said Alice.

"Why, *she*," said the Gryphon. "It's all her fancy, that: they never executes nobody, you know. Come on!"

"Everybody says 'Come on!' here," thought Alice, as she went slowly after it: "I never was so ordered about in all my life, never!"

They had not gone far before they saw the Mock Turtle in the distance, sitting sad and lonely on a little ledge of rock, and, as they came nearer, Alice could hear him sighing as if his heart would break. She pitied him deeply. "What is his sorrow?" she asked the Gryphon. And the Gryphon answered, very nearly in the same

words as before, "It's all his fancy, that: he hasn't got no sorrow, you know. Come on!"

So they went up to the Mock Turtle, who looked at them with large eyes full of tears, but said nothing.

"This here young lady," said the Gryphon, "she wants for to know your history, she do."

"I'll tell it her," said the Mock Turtle in a deep, hollow tone.

"Sit down, both of you, and don't speak a word till I've finished."

So they sat down, and nobody spoke for some minutes. Alice thought to herself "I don't see how he can *ever* finish, if he doesn't begin." But she waited patiently.

"Once," said the Mock Turtle at last, with a deep sigh, "I was a real Turtle."

These words were followed by a very long silence, broken only by an occasional exclamation of "Hjckrrh!" from the Gryphon, and the constant heavy sobbing of the Mock Turtle. Alice was very nearly getting up and saying, "Thank you, Sir, for your interesting story," but she could not help thinking there *must* be more to come, so she sat still and said nothing.

"When we were still little," the Mock Turtle went on at last, more calmly, though still sobbing a little now and then, "we went to school in the sea. The master was an old Turtle—we used to call him Tortoise——"

"Why did you call him Tortoise, if he wasn't one?"[56] Alice asked.

56 A tortoise is, especially in British English, a land or freshwater creature, as distinguished from the sea-going turtle.

"We called him Tortoise because he taught us," said the Mock Turtle angrily. "Really you are very dull!"

"You ought to be ashamed of yourself for asking such a simple question," added the Gryphon; and then they both sat silent and looked at poor Alice, who felt ready to sink into the earth. At last the Gryphon said to the Mock Turtle "Drive on, old fellow! Don't be all day about it!", and he went on in these words:—

"Yes, we went to school in the sea, though you mayn't believe it——"

"I never said I didn't!" interrupted Alice.

"You did," said the Mock Turtle.

"Hold your tongue!" added the Gryphon, before Alice could speak again. The Mock Turtle went on:—

"We had the best of educations—in fact, we went to school every day——"

"*I've* been to a day-school, too," said Alice. "You needn't be so proud as all that."

"With extras?" asked the Mock Turtle, a little anxiously.

"Yes," said Alice: "we learned French and music."

"And washing?" said the Mock Turtle.

"Certainly not!" said Alice indignantly.

"Ah! Then yours wasn't a really good school," said the Mock Turtle in a tone of great relief. "Now, at *ours*, they had, at the end of the bill, 'French, music, *and washing*—extra.' "

"You couldn't have wanted it much," said Alice; "living at the bottom of the sea."

"I couldn't afford to learn it," said the Mock Turtle with a sigh. "I only took the regular course."

"What was that?" inquired Alice.

"Reeling and Writhing, of course, to begin with," the Mock Turtle replied; "and then the different branches of Arithmetic—Ambition, Distraction, Uglification, and Derision."

"I never heard of 'Uglification,'" Alice ventured to say. "What is it?"

The Gryphon lifted up both its paws in surprise. "What! Never heard of uglifying!" it exclaimed. "You know what to beautify is, I suppose?"

"Yes," said Alice doubtfully: "it means—to—make—anything—prettier."

"Well, then," the Gryphon went on, "if you don't know what to uglify is, you *must* be a simpleton."

Alice did not feel encouraged to ask any more questions about it: so she turned to the Mock Turtle, and said "What else had you to learn?"

"Well, there was Mystery," the Mock Turtle replied, counting off the subject on his flappers, "—Mystery, ancient and modern, with Seaography: then Drawling—the Drawling-master was an old conger-eel, that used to come once a week: *he* taught us Drawling, Stretching, and Fainting in Coils."

"What was *that* like?" said Alice.

"Well, I ca'n't show it you, myself," the Mock Turtle said: "I'm too stiff. And the Gryphon never learnt it."

"Hadn't time," said the Gryphon: "I went to the Classical master, though. He was an old crab, *he* was."

"I never went to him," the Mock Turtle said with a sigh. "He taught Laughing and Grief, they used to say."

"So he did, so he did," said the Gryphon, sighing in its turn; and both creatures hid their faces in their paws.

"And how many hours a day did you do lessons?" said Alice, in a hurry to change the subject.

"Ten hours the first day," said the Mock Turtle: "nine the next, and so on."

"What a curious plan!" exclaimed Alice.

"That's the reason they're called lessons," the Gryphon remarked: "because they lessen from day to day."

This was quite a new idea to Alice, and she thought it over a little before she made her next remark. "Then the eleventh day must have been a holiday?"

"Of course it was," said the Mock Turtle.

"And how did you manage on the twelfth?" Alice went on eagerly.

"That's enough about lessons," the Gryphon interrupted in a very decided tone. "Tell her something about the games now."

The Lobster-Quadrille

The Mock Turtle sighed deeply, and drew the back of one flapper across his eyes. He looked at Alice, and tried to speak, but, for a minute or two, sobs choked his voice. "Same as if he had a bone in his throat," said the Gryphon: and it set to work shaking him and punching him in the back. At last the Mock Turtle recovered his voice, and, with tears running down his cheeks, he went on again:—

"You may not have lived much under the sea—" ("I haven't," said Alice)—"and perhaps you were never even introduced to a lobster—" (Alice began to say "I once tasted——" but checked herself hastily, and said "No, never") "——so you can have no idea what a delightful thing a Lobster-Quadrille is!"

"No, indeed," said Alice. "What sort of a dance is it?"

"Why," said the Gryphon, "you first form into a line along the sea-shore——"

"Two lines!" cried the Mock Turtle. "Seals, turtles, and so on: then, when you've cleared the jelly-fish out of the way——"

"*That* generally takes some time," interrupted the Gryphon.

"—you advance twice——"

"Each with a lobster as a partner!" cried the Gryphon.

"Of course," the Mock Turtle said: "advance twice, set to partners——"

"—change lobsters, and retire in same order," continued the Gryphon.

"Then, you know," the Mock Turtle went on, "you throw the——"

"The lobsters!" shouted the Gryphon, with a bound into the air.

"—as far out to sea as you can——"

"Swim after them!" screamed the Gryphon.

"Turn a somersault in the sea!" cried the Mock Turtle, capering wildly about.

"Change lobsters again!" yelled the Gryphon.

"Back to land again, and—that's all the first figure," said the Mock Turtle, suddenly dropping his voice; and the two creatures, who had been jumping about like mad things, sat down again very sadly and quietly, and looked at Alice.

"It must be a very pretty dance," said Alice timidly.

"Would you like to see a little of it?" said the Mock Turtle.

"Very much indeed," said Alice.

"Let's try the first figure!" said the Mock Turtle to the Gryphon. "We can do it without lobsters, you know. Which shall sing?"

"Oh, *you* sing," said the Gryphon. "I've forgotten the words."

So they began solemnly dancing round and round Alice, every now and then treading on her toes when they passed too close, and waving their fore-paws to mark the time, while the Mock Turtle sang this, very slowly and sadly:—

"Will you walk a little faster?" said a whiting to a snail,
"There's a porpoise close behind us, and he's treading on my tail.
See how eagerly the lobsters and the turtles all advance!
They are waiting on the shingle–will you come and join the dance?
Will you, wo'n't you, will you, wo'n't you, will you join the dance?
Will you, wo'n't you, will you, wo'n't you, wo'n't you join the dance?

"You can really have no notion how delightful it will be
When they take us up and throw us, with the lobsters, out to sea!"
But the snail replied "Too far, too far!", and gave a look askance–
Said he thanked the whiting kindly, but he would not join the dance.
Would not, could not, would not, could not, could not join the dance.
Would not, could not, would not, could not, could not join the dance.

"What matters it how far we go?" his scaly friend replied.
"There is another shore, you know, upon the other side..
The further off from England the nearer is to France.
Then turn not pale, beloved snail, but come and join the dance.
Will you, wo'n't you, will you, wo'n't you, will you join the dance?
Will you, wo'n't you, will you, wo'n't you, wo'n't you join the dance?"[57]

57 This parodies the familiar 'The Spider and the Fly,' by Mary Howitt, first published in her SKETCHES OF NATURAL HISTORY *in 1834. The poem opens with an invitation from the rather interesting Spider:*

'Will you walk into my parlour?' said the Spider to the Fly,
''Tis the prettiest little parlour that ever you did spy.'

The Fly at first resists, but its priggish caution is overcome by artful flattery and it becomes the Spider's dinner. The 'dear little children' to whom the poem is addressed are advised to 'take a lesson' from the tale and to avoid 'an evil counsellor.' Wonderland has its own view of which counsellors are evil.

"Thank you, it's a very interesting dance to watch," said Alice, feeling very glad that it was over at last: "and I do so like that curious song about the whiting!"

"Oh, as to the whiting," said the Mock Turtle, "they—you've seen them, of course?"

"Yes," said Alice, "I've often seen them at dinn——" she checked herself hastily.

"I don't know where Dinn may be," said the Mock Turtle; "but, if you've seen them so often, of course you know what they're like?"

"I believe so," Alice replied thoughtfully. "They have their tails in their mouths—and they're all over crumbs."[58]

"You're wrong about the crumbs," said the Mock Turtle: "crumbs would all wash off in the sea. But they *have* their tails in their mouths; and the reason is——" here the Mock Turtle yawned and shut his eyes. "Tell her about the reason and all that," he said to the Gryphon.

"The reason is," said the Gryphon, "that they *would* go with the lobsters to the dance. So they got thrown out to sea. So they had to fall a long way. So they got their tails fast in their mouths. So they couldn't get them out again. That's all."

"Thank you," said Alice, "it's very interesting. I never knew so much about a whiting before."

"I can tell you more than that, if you like," said the Gryphon. "Do you know why it's called a whiting?"

"I never thought about it," said Alice. "Why?"

"*It does the boots and shoes*," the Gryphon replied very solemnly.

Alice was thoroughly puzzled. "Does the boots and shoes!" she repeated in a wondering tone.

"Why, what are *your* shoes done with?" said the Gryphon. "I mean, what makes them so shiny?"

Alice looked down at them, and considered a little before she gave her answer. "They're done with blacking, I believe."

"Boots and shoes under the sea," the Gryphon went on in a deep voice, "are done with whiting. Now you know."

"And what are they made of?" Alice asked in a tone of great curiosity.

"Soles and eels, of course," the Gryphon replied, rather impatiently: "any shrimp could have told you that."

"If I'd been the whiting," said Alice, whose thoughts were still running on the song, "I'd have said to the porpoise 'Keep back, please! We don't want *you* with us!' "

"They were obliged to have him with them," the Mock Turtle said. "No wise fish would go anywhere without a porpoise."

"Wouldn't it, really?" said Alice, in a tone of great surprise.

"Of course not," said the Mock Turtle. "Why, if a fish came to *me*, and told me he was going a journey, I should say 'With what porpoise?' "

"Don't you mean 'purpose'?" said Alice.

"I mean what I say," the Mock Turtle replied, in an offended tone. And the Gryphon added "Come, let's hear some of *your* adventures."

58 Whiting is a small fish with white flesh, apparently marketed in the odd fashion described and cooked in crumbs.

"I could tell you my adventures—beginning from this morning," said Alice a little timidly; "but it's no use going back to yesterday, because I was a different person then."

"Explain all that," said the Mock Turtle.

"No, no! The adventures first," said the Gryphon in an impatient tone: "explanations take such a dreadful time."

So Alice began telling them her adventures from the time when she first saw the White Rabbit. She was a little nervous about it, just at first, the two creatures got so close to her, one on each side, and opened their eyes and mouths so *very* wide; but she gained courage as she went on. Her listeners were perfectly quiet till she got to the part about her repeating *"You are old, Father William,"* to the Caterpillar, and the words all coming different, and then the Mock Turtle drew a long breath, and said "That's very curious!"

"It's all about as curious as it can be," said the Gryphon.

"It all came different!" the Mock Turtle repeated thoughtfully. "I should like to hear her try and repeat something now. Tell her to begin." He looked at the Gryphon as if he thought it had some kind of authority over Alice.

"Stand up and repeat *''Tis the voice of the sluggard,'* " said the Gryphon.

"How the creatures order one about, and make one repeat lessons!" thought Alice. "I might as well be at school at once." However, she got up, and began to repeat it, but her head was so full of the Lobster-Quadrille, that she hardly knew what she was saying; and the words came very queer indeed:—

" 'Tis the voice of the Lobster: I heard him declare
'You have baked me too brown, I must sugar my hair.'
As a duck with his eyelids, so he with his nose
Trims his belt and his buttons, and turns out his toes.
When the sands are all dry, he is gay as a lark,
And will talk in contemptuous tones of the Shark:
But, when the tide rises and sharks are around,
His voice has a timid and tremulous sound."[59]

"That's different from what *I* used to say when I was a child," said the Gryphon.

"Well, *I* never heard it before," said the Mock Turtle; "but it sounds uncommon nonsense."

Alice said nothing; she had sat down with her face in her hands,

59 The last four lines were not in the original ALICE*; they were added in 1886 for the Savile Clark dramatic adaptation. The first four lines parody Carroll's favorite target, Isaac Watts, and his kill-joy poem, 'The Sluggard,' which begins:*

'Tis the voice of the sluggard;
I heard him complain,
'You have wak'd me too soon, I
must slumber again;'
As a door on its hinges, so he on
his bed,
Turns his sides, and his
shoulders, and his heavy head.

Never afraid of repeating himself, Watts adds his favorite moral:

Said I then to my heart, 'Here's
a lesson for me;
This man's but a picture of what
I might be;
But thanks to my friends for their
care in my breeding,
Who taught me betimes to love
working and reading.'

wondering if anything would *ever* happen in a natural way again.

"I should like to have it explained," said the Mock Turtle.

"She ca'n't explain it," hastily said the Gryphon. "Go on to the next verse."

"But about his toes?" the Mock Turtle persisted. "How *could* he turn them out with his nose, you know?"

"It's the first position in dancing," Alice said; but was dreadfully puzzled by it all, and longed to change the subject.

"Go on with the next verse," the Gryphon repeated: "it begins with the words *'I passed by his garden.'* "

Alice did not dare to disobey, though she felt sure it would all come wrong, and she went on in a trembling voice:—

"I passed by his garden, and marked, with one eye,
How the Owl and the Panther were sharing a pie:
The Panther took pie-crust, and gravy, and meat,
While the Owl had the dish as its share of the treat.
When the pie was all finished, the Owl, as a boon,
Was kindly permitted to pocket the spoon:
While the Panther received knife and fork with a growl,
And concluded the banquet by——"[60]

60 This version, an expansion of the original and several intermediate ones, is an improvement on the one first written for the 1886 dramatic adaptation. The original dramatic version included 'eating the Owl' as a conclusion. The poem bears little resemblance to the Watts poem, apart from repeating 'I pass'd by his garden.'

"What *is* the use of repeating all that stuff?" the Mock Turtle interrupted, "if you don't explain it as you go on? It's by far the most confusing thing *I* ever heard!"

"Yes, I think you'd better leave off," said the Gryphon: and Alice was only too glad to do so.

"Shall we try another figure of the Lobster-Quadrille?" the Gryphon went on. "Or would you like the Mock Turtle to sing you another song?"

"Oh, a song, please, if the Mock Turtle would be so kind," Alice replied, so eagerly that the Gryphon said, in a rather offended tone, "Hm! No accounting for tastes! Sing her *'Turtle Soup,'* will you, old fellow?"

The Mock Turtle sighed deeply, and began, in a voice choked with sobs, to sing this:—

"Beautiful Soup, so rich and green,
Waiting in a hot tureen!
Who for such dainties would not stoop?
Soup of the evening, beautiful Soup!

Soup of the evening, beautiful Soup!
Beau—ootiful Soo—oop!
Beau—ootiful Soo—oop!
Soo—oop of the e—e—evening,
Beautiful, beautiful Soup!

"Beautiful Soup! Who cares for fish,
Game, or any other dish?
Who would not give all else for two p
ennyworth only of beautiful Soup?
Pennyworth only of beautiful Soup.
Beau—ootiful Soo—oop!
Beau—ootiful Soo—oop!
Soo—oop of the e—e—evening,
Beautiful, beauti—FUL SOUP!"[61]

61 The original of this parody is 'Beautiful Star,' a song written by J. M. Sayles. The Liddell sisters were prone to sing this song, either through fondness or compulsion; Dodgson records having heard them do so on August 1, 1862. He does not mention the pleasure transmitted by the performance. The original runs:

Beautiful star in heav'n so bright
Softly falls thy silv'ry light,
As thou movest from earth so far,
Star of the evening, beautiful star,

Beau——ti–ful star,
Beau——ti–ful star,
Star——of the eve——ning
Beautiful, beautiful star.

"Chorus again!" cried the Gryphon, and the Mock Turtle had just begun to repeat it, when a cry of "The trial's beginning!" was heard in the distance.

"Come on!" cried the Gryphon, and, taking Alice by the hand, it hurried off, without waiting for the end of the song.

"What trial is it?" Alice panted as she ran; but the Gryphon only answered "Come on!" and ran the faster, while more and more faintly came, carried on the breeze that followed them, the melancholy words:—

"Soo—oop of the e—e—evening,
Beautiful, beautiful Soup!"

XI

Who Stole the Tarts?

The King and Queen of Hearts were seated on their throne when they arrived, with a great crowd assembled about them—all sorts of little birds and beasts, as well as the whole pack of cards: the Knave was standing before them, in chains, with a soldier on each side to guard him; and near the King was the White Rabbit, with a trumpet in one hand, and a scroll of parchment in the other. In the very middle of the court was a table, with a large dish of tarts upon it: they looked so good, that it made Alice quite hungry to look at them—"I wish they'd get the trial done," she thought, "and hand round the refreshments!" But there seemed to be no chance of this; so she began looking about her to pass away the time.

Alice had never been in a court of justice before, but she had read about them in books, and she was quite pleased to find that she knew the name of nearly everything there. "That's the judge," she said to herself, "because of his great wig."

The judge, by the way, was the King; and, as he wore his crown over the wig (look at the frontispiece if you want to see how he did it), he did not look at all comfortable, and it was certainly not becoming.

"And that's the jury-box," thought Alice; "and those twelve creatures," (she was obliged to say "creatures," you see, because some of them were animals, and some were birds,) "I suppose they are the jurors." She said this last word two or three times over to herself, being rather proud of it: for she thought, and rightly too, that very few little girls of her age knew the meaning of it at all. However, "jurymen" would have done just as well.

The twelve jurors were all writing very busily on slates. "What are they doing?" Alice whispered to the Gryphon. "They ca'n't have anything to put down yet, before the trial's begun."

"They're putting down their names," the Gryphon whispered in reply, "for fear they should forget them before the end of the trial."

"Stupid things!" Alice began in a loud, indignant voice; but she stopped hastily, for the White Rabbit cried out "Silence in the court!", and the King put on his spectacles and looked anxiously round, to see who was talking.

Alice could see, as well as if she were looking over their shoulders, that all the jurors were writing down "Stupid things!" on their slates, and she could even make out that one of them didn't know how to spell "stupid," and that he had to ask his neighbour to tell him. "A nice muddle their slates will be in, before the trial's over!" thought Alice.

One of the jurors had a pencil that squeaked. This, of course, Alice could *not* stand, and she went round the court and got behind him, and very soon found an opportunity of taking it away. She did it so quickly that the poor little juror (it was Bill, the Lizard) could not make out at all what had become of it; so, after hunting all about for it, he was obliged to write with one finger for the rest of the day; and this was of very little use, as it left no mark on the slate.

"Herald, read the accusation!" said the King.

On this the White Rabbit blew three blasts on the trumpet, and then unrolled the parchment-scroll, and read as follows:—

"The Queen of Hearts, she made some tarts,
All on a summer day:
The Knave of Hearts, he stole those tarts
And took them quite away!"

"Consider your verdict," the King said to the jury.

"Not yet, not yet!" the Rabbit hastily interrupted. "There's a great deal to come before that!"

"Call the first witness," said the King; and the White Rabbit blew three blasts on the trumpet, and called out "First witness!"

The first witness was the Hatter. He came in with a teacup in one hand and a piece of bread-and-butter in the other. "I beg pardon, your Majesty," he began, "for bringing these in; but I hadn't quite finished my tea when I was sent for."

"You ought to have finished," said the King. "When did you begin?"

The Hatter looked at the March Hare, who had followed him into the court, arm-in-arm with the Dormouse. "Fourteenth of March, I *think* it was," he said.

"Fifteenth," said the March Hare.

"Sixteenth," said the Dormouse.

"Write that down," the King said to the jury; and the jury eagerly wrote down all three dates on their slates, and then added them up, and reduced the answer to shillings and pence.

"Take off your hat," the King said to the Hatter.

"It isn't mine," said the Hatter.

"*Stolen*!" the King exclaimed, turning to the jury, who instantly made a memorandum of the fact.

"I keep them to sell," the Hatter added as an explanation. "I've none of my own. I'm a hatter."

Here the Queen put on her spectacles, and began staring hard at the Hatter, who turned pale and fidgeted.

"Give your evidence," said the King; "and don't be nervous; or I'll have you executed on the spot."

This did not seem to encourage the witness at all: he kept shifting from one foot to the other, looking uneasily at the Queen, and in his confusion he bit a large piece out of his teacup instead of the bread-and-butter.

Just at this moment Alice felt a very curious sensation, which puzzled her a good deal until she made out what it was:

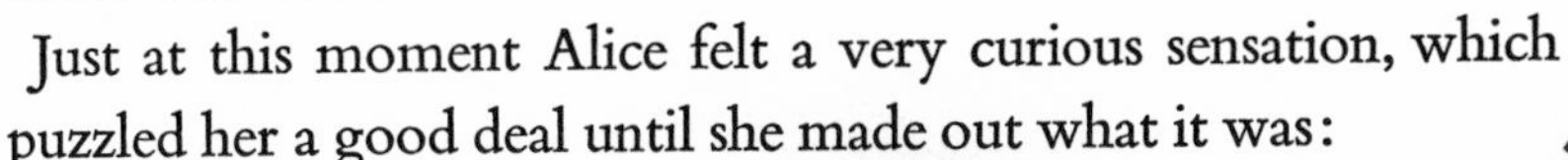

*   *   *   *   *   *   *   *   *   *   *

she was beginning to grow larger again, and she thought at first she would get up and leave the court; but on second thoughts she decided to remain where she was as long as there was room for her.

"I wish you wouldn't squeeze so," said the Dormouse, which was sitting next to her. "I can hardly breathe."

"I ca'n't help it," said Alice very meekly: "I'm growing."

"You've no right to grow *here*," said the Dormouse.

"Don't talk nonsense," said Alice more boldly: "you know you're growing too."

"Yes, but *I* grow at a reasonable pace," said the Dormouse: "not in that ridiculous fashion." And it got up very sulkily and crossed over to the other side of the court.

All this time the Queen had never left off staring at the Hatter,

and, just as the Dormouse crossed the court, she said, to one of the officers of the court, "Bring me the list of the singers in the last concert!" on which the wretched Hatter trembled so, that he shook off both his shoes.

"Give your evidence," the King repeated angrily, "or I'll have you executed, whether you are nervous or not."

"I'm a poor man, your Majesty," the Hatter began, in a trembling voice, "—and I hadn't begun my tea—not above a week or so—and what with the bread-and-butter getting so thin—and the twinkling of the tea——"

"The twinkling of the *what*?" said the King.

"It *began* with the tea," the Hatter replied.

"Of course twinkling *begins* with a T!" said the King sharply. "Do you take me for a dunce? Go on!"

"I'm a poor man," the Hatter went on, "and most things twinkled after that—only the March Hare said——"

"I didn't!" the March Hare interrupted in a great hurry.

"You did!" said the Hatter.

"I deny it!" said the March Hare.

"He denies it," said the King: "leave out that part."

"Well, at any rate, the Dormouse said——" the Hatter went on, looking anxiously around to see if it would deny it too; but the Dormouse denied nothing, being fast asleep.

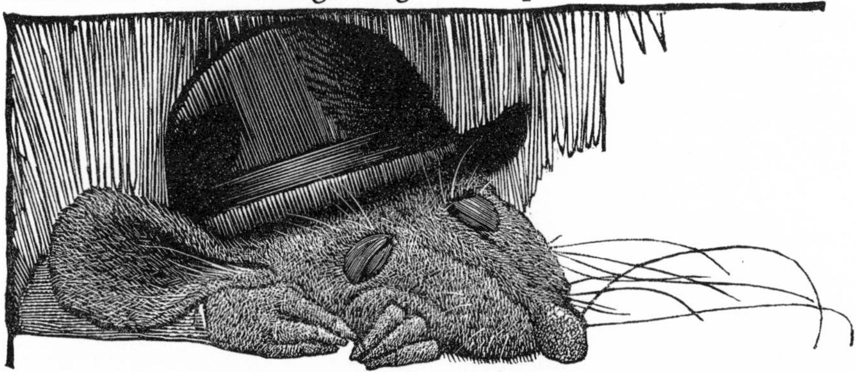

"After that," continued the Hatter, "I cut some more bread-and-butter——"

"But what did the Dormouse say?" one of the jury asked.

"That I ca'n't remember," said the Hatter.

"You *must* remember," remarked the King, "or I'll have you executed."

The miserable Hatter dropped his teacup and bread-and-butter and went down on one knee. "I'm a poor man, your Majesty," he began.

"You're a *very* poor *speaker*," said the King.

Here one of the guinea-pigs cheered, and was immediately suppressed by the officers of the court. (As that is rather a hard word, I will just explain to you how it was done. They had a large canvas bag, which tied up at the mouth with strings: into this they slipped the guinea-pig, head first, and then sat upon it.)

"I'm glad I've seen that done," thought Alice. "I've so often read in the newspapers, at the end of trials, 'There was some attempt at applause, which was immediately suppressed by the officers of the court,' and I never understood what it meant till now."

"If that's all you know about it, you may stand down," continued the King.

"I ca'n't go no lower," said the Hatter: "I'm on the floor, as it is."

"Then you may *sit* down," the King replied.

Here the other guinea-pig cheered, and was suppressed.

"Come, that finishes the guinea-pigs!" thought Alice. "Now we shall get on better."

"I'd rather finish my tea," said the Hatter, with an anxious look at the Queen, who was reading the list of singers.

"You may go," said the King; and the Hatter hurriedly left the court, without even waiting to put his shoes on.

"——and just take his head off outside," the Queen added to one of the officers; but the Hatter was out of sight before the officer could get to the door.

"Call the next witness!" said the King.

The next witness was the Duchess' cook. She carried the pepper-

box in her hand, and Alice guessed who it was, even before she got into the court, by the way the people near the door began sneezing all at once.

"Give your evidence," said the King.

"Sha'n't," said the cook.

The King looked anxiously at the White Rabbit, who said, in a low voice, "Your Majesty must cross-examine *this* witness."

"Well, if I must, I must," the King said with a melancholy air, and, after folding his arms and frowning at the cook till his eyes were nearly out of sight, he said, in a deep voice, "What are tarts made of?"

"Pepper, mostly," said the cook.

"Treacle," said a sleepy voice behind her.

"Collar that Dormouse!" the Queen shrieked out. "Behead that Dormouse! Turn that Dormouse out of court! Suppress him! Pinch him! Off with his whiskers!"

For some minutes the whole court was in confusion, getting the Dormouse turned out, and, by the time they had settled down again, the cook had disappeared.

"Never mind!" said the King, with an air of great relief. "Call the next witness." And, he added, in an undertone to the Queen, "Really, my dear, *you* must cross-examine the next witness. It quite makes my forehead ache!"

Alice watched the White Rabbit as he fumbled over the list, feeling very curious to see what the next witness would be like, "—for they haven't got much evidence *yet*," she said to herself. Imagine her surprise, when the White Rabbit read out, at the top of his shrill little voice, the name "Alice!"

XII

Alice's Evidence

"Here!" cried Alice, quite forgetting in the flurry of the moment how large she had grown in the last few minutes, and she jumped up in such a hurry that she tipped over the jury-box with the edge of her skirt, upsetting all the jurymen on to the heads of the crowd below, and there they lay sprawling about, reminding her very much of a globe of gold-fish she had accidentally upset the week before.

"Oh, I *beg* your pardon!" she exclaimed in a tone of great dismay, and began picking them up again as quickly as she could, for the accident of the gold-fish kept running in her head, and she had a vague sort of idea that they must be collected at once and put back into the jury-box, or they would die.

"The trial cannot proceed," said the King, in a very grave voice, "until all the jurymen are back in their proper places—*all*," he repeated with great emphasis, looking hard at Alice as he said so.

Alice looked at the jury-box, and saw that, in her haste, she had put the Lizard in head downwards, and the poor little thing was waving his tail about in a melancholy way, being quite unable to move. She soon got him out again, and put him right; "not that it signifies much," she said to herself; "I should think he would be *quite* as much use in the trial one way up as the other."

As soon as the jury had a little recovered from the shock of being upset, and their slates and pencils had been found and handed back to them, they set to work very diligently to write out a history of the accident, all except the Lizard, who seemed too much overcome to do anything but sit with his mouth open, gazing up into the roof of the court.

"What do you know about this business?" the King said to Alice.
"Nothing," said Alice.
"Nothing *whatever*?" persisted the King.
"Nothing whatever," said Alice.
"That's very important," the King said, turning to the jury. They were just beginning to write this down on their slates, when the White Rabbit interrupted: "*Un*important, your Majesty means, of course," he said, in a very respectful tone, but frowning and making faces at him as he spoke.
"*Un*important, of course, I meant," the King hastily said, and went on to himself in an undertone "important—unimportant—unimportant—important——" as if he were trying which word sounded best.[62]
Some of the jury wrote it down "important," and some "unimportant." Alice could see this, as she was near enough to look over their slates; "but it doesn't matter a bit," she thought to herself.
At this moment the King, who had been for some time busily writing in his note-book, called out "Silence!", and read out from his book "Rule Forty-two. *All persons more than a mile high to leave the court.*"
Everybody looked at Alice.
"*I'm* not a mile high," said Alice.
"You are," said the King.
"Nearly two miles high," added the Queen.
"Well, I sha'n't go, at any rate," said Alice; "besides, that's not a regular rule: you invented it just now."
"It's the oldest rule in the book," said the King.
"Then it ought to be Number One," said Alice.
The King turned pale, and shut his note-book hastily. "Consider your verdict," he said to the jury, in a low trembling voice.
"There's more evidence to come yet, please your Majesty," said the White Rabbit, jumping up in a great hurry: "this paper has just been picked up."
"What's in it?" said the Queen.
"I haven't opened it yet," said the White Rabbit; "but it seems to be a letter, written by the prisoner to—to somebody."
"It must have been that," said the King, "unless it was written to nobody, which isn't usual, you know."
"Who is it directed to?" said one of the jurymen.
"It isn't directed at all," said the White Rabbit: "in fact, there's

62 *This echoes the Duchess' splendid proverb about attending to sounds and not fretting over meaning. It also recalls, somewhat subversively, Alice's own earlier confusion over the eating habits of cats and bats.*

nothing written on the *outside*." He unfolded the paper as he spoke, and added "It isn't a letter, after all: it's a set of verses."

"Are they in the prisoner's handwriting?" asked another of the jurymen.

"No, they're not," said the White Rabbit, "and that's the queerest thing about it." (The jury all looked puzzled.)

"He must have imitated somebody else's hand," said the King. (The jury all brightened up again.)

"Please your Majesty," said the Knave, "I didn't write it, and they ca'n't prove that I did: there's no name signed at the end."

"If you didn't sign it," said the King, "that only makes the matter worse. You *must* have meant some mischief, or else you'd have signed your name like an honest man."

There was a general clapping of hands at this: it was the first really clever thing the King had said that day.

"That *proves* his guilt, of course," said the Queen: "so, off with——"

"It doesn't prove anything of the sort!" said Alice. "Why, you don't even know what they're about!"

"Read them," said the King.

The White Rabbit put on his spectacles. "Where shall I begin, please your Majesty?" he asked.

"Begin at the beginning," the King said, very gravely, "and go on till you come to the end: then stop."

There was dead silence in the court, whilst the White Rabbit read out these verses:—

"They told me you had been to her,
And mentioned me to him:
She gave me a good character,
But said I could not swim.

He sent them word I had not gone
(We know it to be true):
If she should push the matter on,
What would become of you?

I gave her one, they gave him two,
You gave us three or more;
They all returned from him to you,
Though they were mine before.

If I or she should chance to be
Involved in this affair,
He trusts to you to set them free,
Exactly as we were.

My notion was that you had been
(Before she had this fit)
An obstacle that came between
Him, and ourselves, and it.

Don't let him know she liked them best,
For this must ever be
A secret, kept from all the rest,
Between yourself and me."[63]

"That's the most important piece of evidence we've heard yet," said the King, rubbing his hands; "so now let the jury——"

"If any one of them can explain it," said Alice, (she had grown so large in the last few minutes that she wasn't a bit afraid of interrupting him,) "I'll give him sixpence. *I* don't believe there's an atom of meaning in it."

The jury all wrote down, on their slates, "*She* doesn't believe there's an atom of meaning in it," but none of them attempted to explain the paper.

"If there's no meaning in it," said the King, "that saves a world of trouble, you know, as we needn't try to find any. And yet I don't know," he went on, spreading out the verses on his knee, and looking at them with one eye; "I seem to see some meaning in them, after all. —'*said I could not swim*'— you ca'n't swim, can you?" he added, turning to the Knave.

The Knave shook his head sadly. "Do I look like it?" he said. (Which he certainly did *not*, being made entirely of cardboard.)

"All right, so far," said the King; and he went on muttering over the verses to himself: " '*We know it to be true*'—that's the jury, of course—'*If she should push the matter on*'—that must be the Queen—'*What would become of you?*'—What, indeed!—'*I gave her one, they gave him two*'—why, that must be what he did with the tarts, you know——"

"But it goes on '*they all returned from him to you,*' " said Alice.

"Why, there they are!" said the King triumphantly, pointing to the tarts on the table. "Nothing can be clearer than *that*. Then again

63 *The first version of this, 'She's All My Fancy Painted Him,' was written for one of the family magazines Carroll edited,* MISCH-MASCH, *a German term, we are told, best translated as 'midge-madge' or, more familiarly, 'hodge-podge.' The revision for* ALICE *consists largely in reshuffling the pronouns, without the slightest increase (or decrease) in clarity. The original version began as a parody of a song, 'Alice Gray,' written by William Mee and set to music by Mrs. P. Millard, an extraordinary production which begins:*

She's all my fancy painted her—
Ye Gods! She is divine;
But her heart it is another's—
It never can be mine.

Things do not improve.

—*'before she had this fit'*—you never had *fits*, my dear, I think?" he said to the Queen.

"Never!" said the Queen, furiously, throwing an inkstand at the Lizard as she spoke. (The unfortunate little Bill had left off writing on his slate with one finger, as he found it made no mark; but he now hastily began again, using the ink, that was trickling down his face, as long as it lasted.)[64]

64 Carroll loved to joke with children about ink, offering it to them to drink and sometimes, in letters, playing wild variations on a theme: 'I've got no ink. You don't believe it? Ah, you should have seen the ink there was in MY *days! (About the time of the battle of Waterloo: I was a soldier in that battle.) Why, you had only to pour a little of it on the paper, and it went on by itself!* THIS *ink is so stupid, if you begin a word for it, it can't even finish it by itself.'*

"Then the words don't *fit* you," said the King, looking round the court with a smile. There was a dead silence.

"It's a pun!" the King added in an offended tone, and everybody laughed.

"Let the jury consider their verdict," the King said, for about the twentieth time that day.

"No, no!" said the Queen. "Sentence first—verdict afterwards."

"Stuff and nonsense!" said Alice loudly. "The idea of having the sentence first!"

"Hold your tongue!" said the Queen, turning purple.

"I wo'n't!" said Alice.

"Off with her head!" the Queen shouted at the top of her voice. Nobody moved.

"Who cares for *you*?" said Alice (she had grown to her full size by this time). "You're nothing but a pack of cards!"

At this the whole pack rose up into the air, and came flying down upon her: she gave a little scream, half of fright and half of anger, and tried to beat them off, and found herself lying on the bank, with her head in the lap of her sister, who was gently brushing away some dead leaves that had fluttered down from the trees upon her face.

"Wake up, Alice dear!" said her sister. "Why, what a long sleep you've had!"

"Oh, I've had such a curious dream!" said Alice. And she told her sister, as well as she could remember them, all these strange Adventures of hers that you have just been reading about; and, when she had finished, her sister kissed her, and said "It *was* a curious dream, dear, certainly; but now run in to your tea: it's getting late." So Alice got up and ran off, thinking while she ran, as well she might, what a wonderful dream it had been.

But her sister sat still just as she left her, leaning her head on her hand, watching the setting sun, and thinking of little Alice and all her wonderful Adventures, till she too began dreaming after a fashion, and this was her dream:—

First, she dreamed about little Alice herself: once again the tiny hands were clasped upon her knee, and the bright eager eyes were looking up into hers—she could hear the very tones of her voice, and see that queer little toss of her head to keep back the wandering hair that *would* always get into her eyes—and still as she listened, or seemed to listen, the whole place around her became alive with the strange creatures of her little sister's dream.

The long grass rustled at her feet as the White Rabbit hurried by—the frightened Mouse splashed its way through the neighbouring pool—she could hear the rattle of the teacups as the March Hare and his friends shared their never-ending meal, and the shrill voice of the Queen ordering off her unfortunate guests to execution—once more the pig-baby was sneezing on the Duchess' knee, while plates and dishes crashed around it—once more the shriek of the Gryphon, the squeaking of the Lizard's slate-pencil, and the choking of the suppressed guinea-pigs, filled the air, mixed up with the distant sob of the miserable Mock Turtle.

So she sat on with closed eyes, and half believed herself in Wonderland, though she knew she had but to open them again, and all would change to dull reality—the grass would be only rustling in the wind, and the pool rippling to the waving of the reeds—the rattling teacups would change to tinkling sheep-bells, and the Queen's shrill cries to the voice of the shepherd-boy—and the sneeze of the baby, the shriek of the Gryphon, and all the other queer noises, would change (she knew) to the confused clamour of the busy farm-yard—while the lowing of the cattle in the distance would take the place of the Mock Turtle's heavy sobs.

Lastly, she pictured to herself how this same little sister of hers would, in the after-time, be herself a grown woman; and how she would keep, through all her riper years, the simple and loving heart of her childhood; and how she would gather about her other little children, and make *their* eyes bright and eager with many a strange tale, perhaps even with the dream of Wonderland of long ago; and how she would feel with all their simple sorrows, and find a pleasure in all their simple joys, remembering her own child-life, and the happy summer days.

ALICE'S ADVENTURES IN WONDERLAND

A NOTE ON THE TEXT

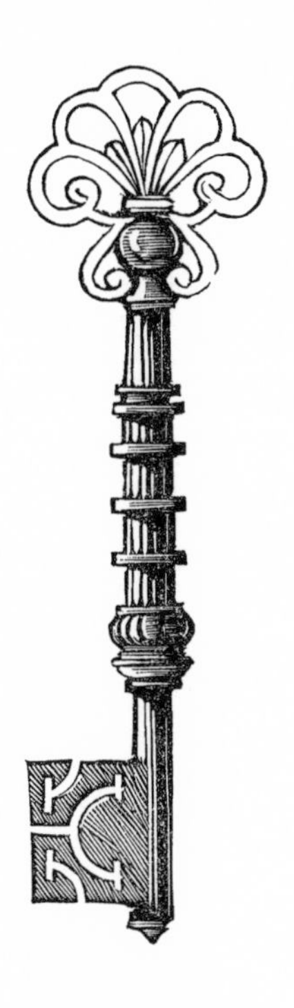

The text for *The Pennyroyal Alice* is essentially an amalgamation of the two revisions to the text that Lewis Carroll supervised in the last 11 years of his life. The first was published in 1887 as the People's Edition, and the second in 1897 as the final revision of the standard "6/- Edition". The two sets of corrections are mostly quite different, but in a few instances different alterations *were* made at the same site; in such cases, we have preferred the later reading.

Many of Lewis Carroll's ideas on printed English were idiosyncratic. A notable example is his use of the contractions "wo'n't", "ca'n't", and "sha'n't" (which are adopted here throughout). He preferred them to the standard "won't", "can't", and "shan't" on the grounds that the apostrophes represent missing letters (he used the conventional "don't" since that has only one letter missing). He went to some lengths in other ways to convert the text to his own theories; the 1897 corrections are well over 400 in number, and it is inevitable that he should have missed certain changes which, according to his own principles, one would have expected him to have made. For this version, we have remedied the deficiencies. These can be summarised:

a. *Capital letter after exclamation.* We have corrected five cases, where this was not done (see, for example, the chorus to the Duchess' song).

b. *Deletion of comma before speech.* Lewis Carroll took great care to do this systematically. Nevertheless, he missed five instances, which we have corrected.

c. *Speech starting with a capital letter.* One instance was missed. We have corrected it.

d. *Spelling changes.* The corrections to the 1897 edition included a number of Carrollian "corrections" (for example, labelled/labeled, down stairs/down-stairs, winter day/winter-day). Lewis Carroll was particularly fond of hyphenations; early in the book, he changes "salt water" to "salt-water", but not when the words appear later. We have changed it. The possessive of "Duchess" is used three times, once as "Duchess' ", twice as "Duchess's". We have preferred the former usage as being easier on the ear.

e. *Colons and semi-colons.* Lewis Carroll's usage of these punctuation marks varies considerably. We have been reticent in altering any, as his guidelines for their use seem so vague. But there are two exceptions – (i) the jousting match with the puppy, which is described in a paragraph of one sentence, with intersections marked by colons – and one semi-colon, which we have altered; (ii) Alice managing her flamingo – a battle that is again punctuated by colons – and one semi-colon, which we have altered.

f. *Other changes of punctuation.* There are a number of minor inconsistencies, which we have rationalised (for example, for "Alice's Right Foot, Esq.," we have added the comma, to suit the address format; 'moral' we have changed to "moral"). We have also corrected a number of minor misprints.

In addition to these "Carrollian" alterations, we have made some changes, which may be viewed as experimental:

a. *Asterisks to denote change of size.* Alice changes size twelve times in Wonderland; three (1, 2 and 7) were originally marked by rows of asterisks. We have marked all twelve changes with asterisks, but in order to distinguish the original from the interpolated, the latter are printed in blue ink, the former in red.

b. *The Mouse's dry history.* The Mouse quotes extensively from Havilland Chepmell's *Short Course of History* (1862). We have taken the liberty of rendering the quotations exact.

c. *Inconsistent gender of certain characters.* It is just possible, though unlikely, that Lewis Carroll intended the inconsistencies, but we think it more likely that he simply did not realise how often he strayed. He was certainly aware of *some* of the inconsistencies, since one of his own 1897 corrections was to alter the Mouse's tail from "his" to "its"; accordingly we have made "him" "it" throughout. In the Trial scene, the Dormouse was changed by Lewis Carroll in 1897 from male to neuter; we have again rationalised the situation by making "him" "it" throughout. For the other characters in question, we have rationalised by keeping to the gender most frequently cited. Thus the White Rabbit, Bill the Lizard, and the March Hare remain "he"; the Gryphon is "it"; and Dinah is "she". We have also feminized the very maternal Canary. We have not altered anywhere where the gender is used in direct speech (unless it is by Alice herself). If the Queen calls the Dormouse "he", then so be it, one does not argue with the Queen.

THE ADDENDA

Christmas-Greetings. The text is taken from the final version published in the 1897 edition of *Through the Looking-Glass,* but with two changes present in the 1897 edition of *Alice's Adventures,* plus the signature (the bibliography of this item is complicated – see "Bibliographical notes on 'Christmas-Greetings'," *Jabberwocky,* Summer 1972).

To all Child-Readers. The text is taken from the pamphlet of 1871. The signature has been changed slightly to conform with the other addenda.

Easter Greeting. The text is taken from the final revised edition of c. 1889, but includes two revisions made for the People's Edition of 1887, plus date and signature.

The Preface to the Eighty-sixth Thousand of the 6/- Edition. [Macmillan, London 1897]. The text is the corrected version of the 1897 edition.

SELWYN H. GOODACRE.
Burton-on-Trent, Staffordshire, November, 1981.

A NOTE ON THE PRINTS

To illustrate *Alice* entails a certain indelicacy, for *Alice* is a story of loneliness. Its illustrators, beginning with Carroll himself and including Tenniel, Rackham, Steadman, Pogany, Furniss, and Dali, have intruded on the privacy of Alice's adventure, standing apart and observing Alice in her dream. They have been voyeurs, and yet there can be no voyeurs to dreams. In *The Pennyroyal Alice*, the reader is a voyeur only when Alice is associated with her sister: first, on the bank; then, after awakening, running home for tea; and finally in her sister's reverie. The images of Alice's dream are always seen from Alice's point of view, for after all, the dream *is* Alice's dream.

I have tried, in every phase of the book's evolution, in both images and design, to be mindful of the text–its spirit, its language, and its calculated pandemonium.

Some of the images seemed to require sources for their details: the Crown of State (the King of Hearts), Queen Victoria's Crown (the Queen of Hearts), the great topiary gardens of Levens Hall and Haseley Court (the Garden), antique poison bottles (DRINK ME), dodos (the Dodo). Other images seemed to call for a quiet disregard of such things, wanting only imagination: the Hatter's watch, the smoke-filled kitchen, the pig-baby, the Mock Turtle.

Carroll's thoughts on his own creation provided important keys which took *The Pennyroyal Alice* in interesting visual directions. For instance, Carroll commented to Alexander Macmillan in 1864 that the binding cloth for *Alice* should be bright red–not because it was the best, he said, but because it would be "the most attractive to childish eyes." I used that note as a displaced chromatic key: red for the shoulder commentary, and red for Alice's name when it is shrieked by the White Rabbit in the trial scene. The blue in the chapter heads and other titles is, of course, Oxford blue. Carroll's letters to and about Tenniel, Arthur Hughes, and G.W. Taylor gave me insights into Carroll's vision of Wonderland, a contradictory vision which embraced the "weird" and "grotesque" as enthusiastically as it embraced the "graceful and pretty."

I have tried to keep the illustrations weird (yet reasonable), and grotesque (yet humorous), but I have not tried to make them pretty or graceful.

I have tried to establish a clean, classic design using traditional typography and rigid, Renaissance margins, yet all the rules and canons I established, I violated–whiskers, hats, fobs, and a mouse's tale come falling and punching, helter skelter, into those carefully pruned margins (after all, in Wonderland, one should never be able to anticipate what's to happen on the next page). Likewise, the traditional typography is chided by the calligraphic whimsy of the title-page and by the unjustified lines. Asymmetry mocks symmetry. Nonsense sullies sense, with appropriate irreverence.

The selection of images evolved slowly, through many readings of the text. Those readings were private for the most part, though I did read it aloud for my daughters' reactions, and I did one thorough reading with James Kincaid. It was in Boulder, with Kincaid, that the notion of the solitary Alice came about. It was he who pointed out the astounding number of times the words "alone" and "lonely" occur.

When Selwyn Goodacre correlated *Alice's* pronouns to the gender of their antecedents, it made me aware of the disproportionate ratio of masculine pronouns to feminine pronouns, a result, I feel certain, of the masculine Victorianism of which Carroll and Oxford were a part. It is fitting that Alice be confronted with a preponderance of male characters – threatening, curious, pitiful.

After a few false starts, I began a full sequence of the initial studies for the seventy-five engravings. I based their compositions on the typographic page and completed them in two days. I wanted them to spill out as rapidly as possible. I wanted them all to breathe with the same breath. It may also interest the reader to know that the seventy-five prints herein, plus thirty or so rejected blocks, were engraved in little over four months, from 10 August to 20 December, 1981. As George Bernard Shaw said, "only whiskey makes it possible."

Finally I would like to offer, for enjoyment's sake only, a few random notes about specific prints, especially those in the fore and after matter.

The keys are, of course, variants on the Golden key (p.42). They are the keys to the Garden, which Alice pictures as a sane refuge in a wonderland of insanity. They are used, in mirrored pairs, as decorative devices.

The floral motifs are also decorative in intent, though there is a symbolic relationship between the flower and the addendum it accompanies. The holly wreath ("A Christmas-Greeting") is obvious. So is the wreath of daisies ("All in the Golden Afternoon") that frames the Tower of "the House." The Pomegranate ("Easter Greeting") is a traditional symbol for the Resurrection of Christ, the "unseen Friend" Carroll remembers to his child-friends. The grapevine ("To All Child-Readers"), also a symbol for Christ, is taken from St. John's Gospel, the fifteenth chapter. Aconitum ("Eighty-sixth Thousand of the 6/- Edition.") is, for contrast, an hallucinogen which is associated with transmogrifications and seems somehow to befit a riddle.

I modeled the Mad Hatter after my dear friend Allen Mandelbaum, having been taken by his wonderful madness and the striking array of hats in his Manhattan apartment.

It has been suggested on numerous occasions that Richard Nixon was the model for the Duchess. Though I did not intend such a parody, the idea is not without merit. Indeed, it echoes Carroll's words: "a book should always mean a great deal more than the writer (illustrator) intended."

As for Alice's model, I chose my own dark-eyed daughter of ten who bears a shocking resemblance to Alice Liddel, and whose hair not only "wants cutting" but does "always get into her eyes."

The Cheshire Cat is modeled after the hairless Sphinx, a ridiculously rare feline, which like a mule cannot reproduce itself.

BARRY MOSER.
Hatfield, Massachusetts.

ACKNOWLEDGEMENTS

Pennyroyal Press would like to acknowledge the generous assistance rendered by the following friends and colleagues: Richard Altick, Donald Baker, Edward Guiliano, Larry Hunt, Anita Kincaid, John Lancaster, Julian Markels, Cara Moser, Michael Preston, Charles Proudfit, J. E. Rivers, Richard Schoeck, Alan Scheinman, and P. Chase Twichell.

Special thanks to Jeffrey Dwyer, the financial architect of this project and to the partnerships of Robert Abuza, Joseph DeFazio, Janet Rowe Dugan, Arnold Elkind, Richard Gangel, Betty Horton, Elizabeth Hunt, J. E. Lunny, Laury Magnus, Jay Readinger & Glenn Swanson, Alfred Regan, John P. Regish, Raymond R. Rex Jr., David Schaefer, Jacob Schulman, R. S. Varady, George Whitney, and Amos Zeidman.

And to Allen Mandelbaum, whose large energy & larger heart brought this coalition into being—

Aoleus rushes with his winds, / The lizard darts, / but neither Aoleus nor the lizard / is as dashing as the Hoarse Savant...
& off we go

This edition of

ALICE'S ADVENTURES IN WONDERLAND

is a slightly modified reproduction of the original printing by Harold McGrath at Pennyroyal Press, West Hatfield, Massachusetts. The type is Monotype Bembo and Bembo Italic, with Alfred Fairbanks' Condensed Italic and John Peters' Castellar, here reproduced at approximately three-quarters original size. The original typography was composed and cast at the type foundry of Winifred and Michael Bixler, Boston; with considerable hand composition being done entirely by Arthur Larson at the Pennyroyal Press. The calligraphy on the title page is the work of G. G. Laurens, as is the versal 'A' of the first chapter opening. The separations for the wood engravings were done by Bright Arts (Singapore) Pte. Ltd. The book was printed at Holyoke Lithograph, Springfield, Massachusetts, and bound at Book Press, Inc., Brattleboro, Vermont.

ALICE'S ADVENTURES IN WONDERLAND

For Our Children